HER GENTLEMAN PIRATE

High Seas & High Stakes Series

TAMARA GILL

Her Gentleman Pirate
High Seas & High Stakes Series
Novella Two

Copyright 2016 by Tamara Gill
Cover Art by EDH Graphics

This book is a work of fiction. The names, characters, places, and incidents are products of the writer's imagination or have been used fictitiously and are not to be construed as real. Any resemblance to persons, living or dead, actual events, locales or organizations is entirely coincidental.

All rights reserved. Without limiting the rights under copyright reserved above, no part of this publication may be reproduced, stored in or introduced into a database and retrieval system or transmitted in any form or any means (electronic, mechanical, photocopying, recording or otherwise) without the prior written permission of both the owner of copyright and the above publishers.

ISBN-13: 9781980767671

DEDICATION

This book is for all my loyal readers out there who love adventure on the high seas.

CHAPTER 1

Valletta Harbor, Malta – 1819

"Take her aboard and place her in my cabin. And make sure you tie her up. Tight. She's a bit of a hoyden this one, make no mistake." A deep, rough voice said from behind her.

Lady Arabella Hester, normally a serene woman, growled. A most unladylike sound if ever there was one to be sure, but what was she to do with a dirty piece of cloth tied across her mouth? To be kidnapped was not something she'd ever thought to happen while visiting Malta with her papa, they had many friends, certainly no one that wished them ill, or so she thought…

She shivered as the night air pierced her thin shift, having been pulled from her bed. The lapping sound of water sounded beneath her feet, and Arabella knew she was at the docks. This was a rightful catastrophe!

The captain, bastard extraordinaire grinned and again Arabella was forced into an action beyond reprehensible. She spat on his old, sea-worn boot. He would pay for kidnapping her and possibly ruining her good name should anyone find out. Which no doubt was his aim or worse, to do unthinkable things to her that even she didn't want to face right at this moment.

She tried to squirm free of her captor, standing too close against her back and then, like a sack of potatoes, was flung over the deckhands' shoulders, carried unceremoniously onto the boat, off the main deck and supposedly toward the captain's cabin.

The wooden ships interior oozed with the smell of unwashed men and stale air. Her nose twitched at the rank odor that wafted up from the man carrying her. Did these men have no pride? There was plenty of water about; one would think a wash every few days wouldn't be so hard.

He threw her into a chair and her bottom roared in protest. She tried to rub her sore hide, before he wrenched her hands behind the chair and tied them firmly to the wood.

Arabella fought against the knots, landing at least one solid kick to the captor's shin. He glared at her, but didn't retaliate with violence. "You'll all pay for this absurdity. My father and betrothed will not stand for such foolhardy actions. You will all hang."

Her words only ventured a tighter knot about her ankles. She refused to cringe as the harsh rope bit into her flesh. She glared at the bulk of a man who strode off without a flicker of remorse. The door slammed shut and her imprisonment was complete.

Her eyes burned and she bit her lip to stop the tears from welling and falling over her lids. There wasn't time for emotion. Crying couldn't possibly help her situation. A gun would be handy, yes, but not a blabbering little fool that was threatening to come out and make it's presence known. Arabella took a calming breath and fought to think clearly. Her father would look for her, chase down this pirate and ensure justice, she was sure of it. Her papa, a savvy business man knew everyone who traded on the seas. It would not be long before he found out who'd taken her and rescue her in turn. All she had to do was remain calm and dissuade her captors to do anything beyond forgiving.

She took in the room, which was large for a pirate vessel. Not that she'd ever been on one before to judge. It was also shockingly tidy and clean of dust and grime. It certainly smelt better in here than out in the other part of below decks. A large wooden bed sat against one wall, a desk that if she turned her head a little, could be seen behind her shoulder. Large windows ran the length of the ship's stern. They would give a wonderful view of the ocean should she be able to see out of them, and only *if* she wanted to that was.

Not that she would want to see her island holiday home of Malta disappear over the horizon. At the thought of leaving a place that for the last three months had brought happiness to her and her papa after the passing of her mother, tore pain through her chest. Not to mention society would shun her after this ruination, even the limited London society in which she graced. Her life was just about to start. She was only twenty, it couldn't be over already.

She pulled against her bonds with little luck.

Hurried footsteps sounded coming toward the door and her stomach knotted tighter than those about her ankles. The footsteps paused momentarily at the threshold, before the man she would remember for the rest of her days flung open the door, leaned against the wood and stared at her like a prized jewel.

And that was exactly what she was to him. Coin.

"You'll hang for this, you bastard." The vulgarity of

her speech made her pause, but then she couldn't regret it. If ever there was a time for swearing, this was it.

He laughed and slammed the door shut. "I very much hope you're wrong, Miss Arabella." He studied her a moment, his visage one of annoyance and contemplation. "I can call you Arabella, may I not? We are after all going to be spending some time with each other and I do hate standing on ceremony when there is really no need to. I'm Captain Blackmore, but you may call me Stephen."

Arabella narrowed her eyes but refrained from replying. She needed to remain composed, talk herself out of this situation if possible, not annoy the man any more than he already was, having succumbed to such tactics as kidnapping.

"You see, my dear, I perceive no fun to be had at the end of a noose." One side of his lips lifted in a cocky grin and she took a calming breath. "In any case, if you're worried your virginity will be in tatters after I'm through with you, you'll be sadly mistaken. You shall leave this ship in good time, hale and whole. I promise you that." He rubbed his jaw and she noted he had lovely cheekbones for a pirate, before throwing the thought aside. "Your reputation may suffer though I'm afraid... Society can be so fickle, don't you agree?"

A thread of peace flowed through her and his no-nonsense speech. Perhaps there was hope in talking this pirate out of his idea for her. "You need to think about what you're doing and who you're doing it to. And let me assure you, I am a lady and one who has done nothing to deserve this. And do not doubt that just because I am female I do not hold the lofty connections in which to sink this piece of rubble to the bottom of the ocean." Arabella reminded herself she was supposed to be diplomatic, not demonic. "I don't understand why you've chosen me as your victim. I've done nothing to you. I don't even know you." She stated. Perhaps somewhere deep inside this man, there was an honest soul.

He looked down at her over his nose, the gaze mocking. "You may not have done anything to me but someone close to you has. You, Miss Hester, are imperative to my plans. But," he said, coming to stand not far from her, running an idle hand atop his chest of drawers as if to feel the smooth wood. "For now, all you need to know is that these quarters will be your home over the forthcoming weeks and you'll share them with me. Do not try and escape for the only way to do so would be to swim. And I will not be bothered nor do I have the time to fish you out of the ocean should you choose to try your luck. Do you understand?"

She ground her teeth. The urge to tell this kidnapper what he could do with his threats almost overcame her sense of self-preservation. How dare he speak to her in such a way? Then, what was she thinking. Pirates, men who marched to their own illegal drum would never see reason. They only thought of themselves, and not what their actions meant for others. "You can go to hell. To do this to a woman who has in no way injured you makes your heart as black as this ship." And his hair, which was strikingly long as well, and looked wind kissed. Arabella studied his features for a moment, his strong jaw, the severe cut of his cheekbones and blue intelligent eyes spoke of breeding and an affluent lifestyle. He looked as though he belonged in a London ballroom, dancing with the upper-ten-thousand, not here on a ship, kidnapping innocent women as a means to get what he wanted.

He shrugged, walking toward a wooden sideboard and pouring himself a brandy from the decanter. "I'm owed a debt that will be paid. You are worth a lot of blunt, so do be obliging, my dear. I hate conflict."

Arabella fought against her ties to no avail. He watched her for a moment, a laughing light in his eyes, before turning and leaving her alone in the room.

The ship rocked, the ocean lulling her to a false sense of security.

These men were dangerous. Had in fact stolen her in the dead of night from a family friends estate in Valletta. Arabella looked about the room. What was it exactly that had happened to this pirate to ensure such wrath. It certainly wasn't fair to drag her into his financial woes. But again, she'd been told of these men on their boat trip over to Malta, of how they operated and their lack of conscience.

She made one final effort to free herself and then gave up. It was no use and the sting about her wrists only told her to continue the fight would lead to severe scaring. Arabella shut her eyes, her body aching with the need to sleep. Having been bundled into a rough, hessian bag, thrown into a carriage and stowed on a ship's deck had left her near exhausted.

After losing her mama to a wasting disease, they had needed to get away from London. Everything at home had reminded them both of what they'd loved and lost. With the warmth of the Mediterranean sun, each day on Malta had brought Arabella and her papa back to life. She'd become engaged to a man who would elevate their family, and it was a match that would've made her mama happy. Everything had been falling into place.

But no more. Society would shun her family once they found out about her abduction, another blow that her papa could not take. Tears fell onto her shift and she closed her eyes, blocking out the terrible situation she now found herself, but it was no use. No denying of her location could change where she now was.

Muffled sounds from the deck above floated through to her, calls to hoist the main sail, steer toward starboard gradually faded as sleep crept over her.

A welcome respite and one she hoped she would wake from only to find this nightmare was nothing but a figment of her imagination.

It was not.
Arabella woke with a start as the cabin door slammed against the wall. The pirate captain Blackmore strode in, walked to his dresser and started looking through other articles of clothing.

She blinked and her mouth popped open at the defined, enhancing muscles that accentuated his shoulders and perfect back. His skin was tanned and smooth and dripping with water as if he'd just bathed. From this distance, it looked supple yet flexed with months of tough work aboard a ship's deck.

Illegal work…

He turned and her stomach twisted. The pirate's front was even more defined if that was at all possible. He watched her under heavy eyelids as he pulled on the plain cotton shirt, tying it closed from the chest up. The silly shirt clung to his body and even with him clothed, it did little to hide his form.

Arabella shook herself free from the absurd thoughts running through her mind. Thoughts that included wondering what he looked like without his well-worn breeches on. Was his bottom as toned as his abdomen? Did he wear drawers under his breeches? "You're doing your shirt up wrong. A man of your advanced age should know how to dress himself."

He grinned and looked down at his lopsided tying. "I like doing things that are not *proper*."

The way he accentuated the word *proper* with a look that spoke of endless nights of sin within his arms made her cheeks burn. She scoffed. "Why doesn't that surprise me?" Arabella focused on anything in the room, so long as it was not this wet shirt, heathen before her. He was making her mind addled and as foggy as the moors in winter.

"By the way, to the lady who knows all regarding dressing, but has probably never dressed herself once in her life. I am nine and twenty, so not into my dotage quite yet." He came and sat on the desk, his body looming over hers in the chair.

The smell of ocean wafted from his skin. Surprisingly it wasn't an awful scent although she made a point of gasping for air. "Please move. You smell as rotten as your soul."

"I shouldn't stink at all. I've just bathed which I'm sure you've already surmised. You were after all, quite focused on me as I dressed."

Arabella quickly glanced at him and cursed her foolishness as soon as she did so. She rolled her eyes, knowing too well she'd noticed such things, of how his cheeks were clean-shaven and smooth, his hair recently brushed. She fisted her hands against a scheming pirate she ached to slap. "You should've used soap; water is not enough in your case."

He narrowed his eyes. "And you should know when to speak and when not to. As a reward for your insolent tongue, and the fact you're so well versed in dressing, I'm going to allow you to assist me from now on. When you've learnt to behave and not try to escape of course."

Arabella laughed, the sound dripping with sarcasm. "I will never help you dress and I will never stop trying to get away from you either. No matter what the risk may be to my life. You're a fiend and one who will pay for this folly with *his* life. I promise you that." Not that Arabella knew how she'd accomplish such a thing, but she would try none-the-less.

He shrugged, seemingly unperturbed. "There is no way out of this room unless you like to swim. So I need you to promise me that if I relent and remove your bonds, you will stay where you are and not cause any strife? You're going to be with us for some weeks, Arabella. It would be best if you just accepted the fact you're my prisoner until I deem that no longer necessary."

Arabella glared. "Of course I'll stay here," she said, losing patience. "I don't believe I would enjoy drowning." She paused for breath. "But rest assured, at the first opportune moment, I will be gone."

He grinned. "I do not doubt you will try."

She gasped as he reached around her and slit the ropes free from her hands. His breath whispered against her cheek and shivers raced down her spine. He stood back and once more she could breathe.

He then cut the bonds about her ankles. "You may thank me now." He stood and looked down at her like an errant child who refused to do as they were told. "You know, for a lady you lack manners."

Arabella growled at his retreating back. Losing control of her temper, she stood, picked up the glass blotter from his desk and threw it at his head. She missed, her aim off by an embarrassingly large amount of feet.

He smiled as she reached for the ink jar, the gesture

lighting up his eyes and drawing her in to his deep blue depths to flounder. Why couldn't *something* on the man be awful and ugly?

No. Not Captain Blackmore it would seem.

"Please don't throw any more of my things," he said, grinning. "I'm quite fond of them and I'd hate to have to punish you."

The jar smashed beside his head spilling ink down the wooden walls and splattering a little over his newly worn shirt. Arabella smirked. No one would dictate to her, especially a scoundrel kidnapper. "I do apologize, captain. My hand slipped."

※

Stephen bolted the door shut and leaned against it. He smiled at Lady Arabella Hester's antics and swearing that continued behind the wooden walls. He had to concede, she was very strong willed. And right now, she hated him. After spilling ink on his last good shirt, he'd promptly tied her back up and threatened again to place a bandana over her mouth. It had quietened her for a minute or so, but that was it.

He headed up to the quarter deck. The day was clear, not a cloud darkened the sky. His men went about their jobs without the need for him to tell them what to do or when to do it. Life was good. His plan had worked and soon the two thousand pounds he was owed would be stowed below decks in lieu of his prisoner.

Stephen went back up on deck and walked toward the wheel, taking over from his helmsman. The wind caught the main sail and their speed increased. The island of Malta was no longer visible and he was thankful of it. The further they travelled from the island the better. Lady

Arabella's father would have already dispatched men to save his daughter and her delicate reputation. He needed to make England, London in fact, and fast. It was the only way he'd be able to disappear into the city and keep her safe until the debt owed was paid in full. He had enough friends to keep his location safe, and movable about the city without detection.

"How's the captive?"

Stephen met his helmsman's gaze. "Annoyed. I'd always assumed ladies were of delicate impositions and lightly spoken. This one is an exception to that rule. Her vocabulary, or her preference toward the word *bastard* is enough to make the ladies of her society have an attack of the vapors."

Not to mention how damn beautiful she looked when firing insults against his head. Her brown locks, hanging loose about her shoulders, lips that were plump and just begging for his own to smash against them. Days before he'd kidnapped Arabella, he'd watched her from afar. Her infectious laughter with her friends had often brought a smile to his face. And from a distance he'd noted her height, but even he was shocked to learn her perfect button nose reached his chin. Which brought to mind how long her legs were and since the day he'd thrown her in to his cabin how much he'd enjoy the feel of them wrapped about his waist.

His man chuckled. "You jest." He paused. "In truth Captain, how is she? Do you think she'll try and escape, or cause trouble?"

"I think if she could get her hand on a gun she'd shoot me right dead. But no matter. The little minx will eventually realize she's stuck with us no matter what she tries. Until Sir Hester pays up at least."

Stephen adjusted the wheel and raised his face to the

sun. What a fabulous day this was turning out to be. Below his very feet, he had his blunt, feisty as ever and safely stowed in his cabin, while before him, his crew worked hard and were sailing for England.

Not his first choice, Scotland would suit him better, but he'd not had the pleasure to call it his ancestral country home. Thanks to his great-grandfather having lost everything on a turn of a card, or so the old tale went. Time to accept his situation and make the best of his life.

"What will you do if her father refuses to pay you what he owes? We've never killed before and some of the men are raising concerns over your actions, Captain."

Stephen frowned. The last thing he'd wished to do was upset his crew, but after months of broken promises of payment, he'd had to act. He couldn't be seen as weak. All of his crew would be in danger if such a rumor leaked out across the oceans. And it had only taken one look of the chit and he'd known what he would do...

"You have my word I'll not kill her, but I will ruin her should payment not be forthwith. I'll make it well known it was me who'd kept her onboard my ship for months... unchaperoned. By tarnishing her reputation, I diminish her father's good name with it."

His man shuffled his feet looking paler than normal. Stephen's patience faltered.

"Captain, you're not going to rape her? We may be smugglers, pirates perhaps who don't always confirm to the laws of man, but none of us are so unsavory. We have wives, families to care for." He cleared his throat. "None of us wish to swing at the end of a noose for this chit."

"And you will not. That I can promise you. Her father will pay and that will be the end of it."

"I hope so, Captain."

Stephen handed him the wheel and walked about the

deck for a time thinking over his men's concerns. Should Sir Hester refuse to pay, his life on the sea would continue for a few more years yet. It wasn't in his plan. The small castle he'd bought and paid for in Scotland required extensive repairs and the funds owed were going to ensure that happened. For the first time in his life, his mother would live in the station to which she should've been born. Not in a fisherman's cottage in Cornwall. His great-grandfather's recklessness with blunt had secured their fate and he'd done all that he could to make his mother's life as comfortable as possible while she waited for him to become a self-made man.

But it wasn't enough. He wanted what was taken from him by no fault of his own. He had gentleman blood in his veins, and god damn it, he'd die with the life of one if it was the last thing he did.

CHAPTER 2

The kidnapping pirate had forgotten about her.

For three days he'd left her to wander his cabin, spend every hour enclosed in a space she'd walked around a million times. At least the captain had thought to give her some essentials for her stay. Like a privacy screen, a jug and bowl for bathing and two gowns, even if they were three seasons old, at least they were clean. She'd been able to open a small window to allow the fresh sea air to enter, too small to crawl through unfortunately, but what she really desired was sunlight. And lots of it.

The scrape of her breakfast tray being placed on the floor before her door made her stomach rumble. Today, instead of the ruffian cook she was used to greeting with disdain, this morning the captain himself brought her breakfast.

Good. Maybe she could tip it on his head.

"Your breakfast." He placed it on his desk and stood, legs apart and arms crossed over his chest. A chest barely hidden beneath the half-open shirt he wore. Skin touched by the sun peeked out at her, tempting her to feel the contoured lines that made up his body.

Arabella shook herself from imagining what he'd feel like. She didn't want to touch him, or be anywhere near the pirate if she could help it. "I suppose I should thank you, but I won't. What do you want?"

His lips quirked before he chuckled, showing his straight, lovely teeth. She cursed. "You can thank me in other ways."

"Really, and what do you suggest I do?" Arabella poured herself a cup of tea and took a sip. The beverage went some way in dispelling her bad mood, but not by much. How dare he want thanks from her? She didn't ask to be here, he was holding her captive. It was his duty to keep her from starving.

"After you have broken your fast you're required on deck."

"What?" The tea splashed over her hand and she put the cup down with a clatter. "You're letting me outside? How long are you allowing me this treat? Please tell me it's a day at least."

"That will depend on you. I will see you outside shortly."

Arabella smiled. Sunlight. Oh how she'd missed it and now if she behaved herself she could spend a whole day lazing around on deck enjoying it. She tried to think if she'd seen a chair she could procure while out there so to enjoy the marvelous ocean.

She quickly finished her breakfast, tidied her appearance as best she could considering she was wearing day's old clothing and headed up on deck. When she stepped out into the corridor, Arabella was pleased to note no one stood guard to stop her.

The brightness of the sun after days of being stuck

indoors made her squint. Men stopped what they were doing and stared, some looking less savory than others. She glared at them, lifted her nose and walked toward the bow and the magnificent view that opened out before her.

Footsteps sounded behind and she turned. The captain strode toward her. Awareness shivered down her spine at the determined glint she read in his eyes. His hungry gaze raked over her and she swallowed. Hard. "Thank you for letting me on deck." Arabella looked about. "Is there a chair or stool about that I may use for the day?"

His deep rumbling laugh caused her stomach to twist.

"What's so funny?" she asked, annoyed.

"Beside the fact you expect to sit on deck and lounge about while my men work hard for their captain. Nothing at all entertaining about that." The words dripped sarcasm.

"You're not my captain, which I'm sure I need not remind you. You kidnapped me, remember?"

"Aye, I kidnapped you and for good reason, but now you need to work. I don't accept laziness from my crew and that goes for the women whose family is in debited to me. You must work for your upkeep, room and food." He pulled a wooden pole from behind his back with an array of cotton tassels on one end. Arabella frowned at the apparatus having never seen anything similar in her life.

"What is that?" She stepped back, the hard wooden railing pushing against her spine.

"This is a mop and that bucket on the ground over there is what you're going to use to wash my deck. All of it."

Arabella stared at the bucket filled with soapy water. "I will not. I think you're forgetting who I am."

"And who is that?" he asked, an amused grin on his face.

"I'm a lady and ladies do not clean pirate's ships." Arabella's temper rose with the continual laughing expression on his face. She clenched her hand to stop herself from slapping his cheek.

He passed her the so-called mop ignoring her protests entirely. Arabella snatched it out of his hands. "I'm not cleaning your boat."

"It's a ship. And yes, you are."

"Really." She faced the sea then pitched the cleaning apparatus overboard. That she'd denied him the pleasure of seeing her mop his deck like some scullery maid filled her with pride. She turned to him and smiled. "Oh dear, I seem to have dropped it."

He stared at her, his expression seemingly one of surprise and then contemplation. "There is a punishment for disobeying a captain's order." His tone was low, deadly and all amusement vanished from his face.

Arabella's stomach clenched. The word *punishment* didn't sound at all like something she wanted to experience. Did it involve physical abuse? Would he give her to his crew for enjoyment? Would he touch her himself? The thought sent panic spiraling through her limbs making them weak. "What are you going to do to me?"

He called out to one of his deckhands, the man scrambling over as quickly as he could to his captain. "Go to the galley and grab another mop. Miss Hester has misplaced the one kept up here."

"Yes, Captain," the young man said, before hurrying away.

"I dislike you immensely." She took in the size of the ship and the amount of wood she was supposed to clean. It was an impossible duty for her to fulfill and something about the captain's smirk told her he knew exactly what she was thinking. How could he do this to a woman who'd never cleaned in her life. If she did it wrong, which was highly likely, would he make her do it again? It wasn't to be borne.

Not wanting to spike his ire any more today less he throw her back in his room, as soon as the replacement apparatus was handed to her, she set out to finish the job. If by chance this mop went overboard by the end of the cleaning it was not her fault. Accidents happen...

Hours passed, the captain the entire time never far away, watching her every move, the heat of his gaze making her skin prickle more than the sun on her skin. The muscles in her arms burned with overuse and sweat dripped between places sweat should never drip. In no way had she ever been made to work so hard in her life. Should society see her now, hair limp about her face, her dress ruined by grime, her fingers bruised and bleeding, she would never be allowed back in the glittering ballrooms of the *ton*.

Not that that would tax her too much. Society had never drawn her like so many other ladies of her class. There was no adventure, no chance of a grand love just waiting for her across a supper room table. Her life, just as her father wished it to be, was full of order and conformity. And her betrothed was exactly like him. She scrubbed harder against the wood, her life like the ocean before her, a never-ending swirl of boring. Although she had to admit the ocean wasn't always so calm and peaceful.

When she'd met Lord Frederick Montague, a viscount with large holdings in Somerset, for the first time her life seemed complete. He would love her immediately, be gallant and kiss her senseless.

He did not.

Instead, he'd looked at her like she'd sported some beastly bug on her face, sniffed and continued to talk to the gentleman beside him at the dinner table as if she didn't exist. And for the few weeks he'd graced their life in Valletta she hadn't been his priority. Lord Montague had gone about his days making sure to stay well away from her and ensuring no more than a good morning and good night was spoken. To just image her betrothed coming to save her was absurd.

He was ridiculous and there was nothing she could do about it. She scrubbed the deck harder. The contract was signed and her father overjoyed. And as much as Arabella loved her papa and wished to make him happy, something told her the moment she married Lord Montague she would never be so again.

Arabella huffed out a breath. Visiting Malta had had its advantages and her time there had enabled her heart to heal a little after losing her dear mama. Although the society was large enough to house fabulous balls and entertainments during the Season, it also left a lot of time to fill. Over the weeks of their stay she'd become friends with a daughter from a local family who graced the same social sphere. Nina, or Miss Rowsley had often attended the nightly parties with her and helped her sneak out a time or two to mask balls that they were forbidden to attend.

She would miss her friend dearly and she knew who to blame for that.

She stopped to have a break, and her attention was pulled to where the captain stood steering the ship. His muscled arms flexed with their task, his upper body bared to the elements and bronzed by the sun.

The urge to lick her lips like a droplet of him was sitting there fought with her self-control. She didn't like this man any more than she liked her betrothed. Although, she had to admit, at least the captain spoke to her. It was more than Lord Montague had ever done.

She studied him for a moment. Reveled in the power his presence exhibited. A queer flutter took flight in her belly and for the first time in her life, Arabella wondered what it would be like to lay with a man.

The thought pulled an array of others with it. Like how many women *had* he seduced. Did he have a special woman waiting for him somewhere? Did he find Arabella attractive or only a means to an end?

Their gazes locked and her mouth dried. His intense stare sizzled the space separating them and under no circumstance could she shift her attention elsewhere. From the short distance between them he took in her every feature. His inspection left little to the imagination. Heat bloomed up her neck and she turned to look out over the ocean.

He was a rogue through and through and one that with just one look could make her forget who she was and what he'd done to her.

Worse, Arabella had a feeling he could also make her forget the society in which she was born with just one touch.

CHAPTER 3

She was tied up again.

Arabella sighed. It seemed throwing the captain's second mop and bucket overboard had pushed the man too far. But never would she allow him to make her do such a menial task again. Her arms still ached, a fact that wasn't helped with them being tied behind her back.

The sun had long gone down and her stomach rumbled, reminding her of the late hour. She was being punished. Dinner had not been forthcoming and the thought of missing out brought tears to her eyes. Would he feed her at all tonight?

Gosh she hoped so.

She glanced over his desk and spied the apple sitting on a tray. Not being able to reach for it made her stomach cramp even more. The captain would pay for this abuse.

Wiggling her bonds was of little use and so she sat and waited for when he decided to turn up. If ever. Laughter and loud jests sounded from the deck above. Someone played a pipe instrument of some sort that made these sea fearing men dance, if the loud steps were anything to go by.

It was obvious that in their enjoyment they'd forgotten about her. Were content to let her starve to death.

The door opened and she almost sighed in relief, but the severe set of the captain's face soon stopped all mirth. His eyes were sleepy, a day's growth of beard marked his strong jaw. Arabella swallowed the trepidation that took flight in her gut. He was foxed. Her attention snapped to his bared torso and the corded muscles that flexed with each breath.

She should look away with disdain. She was a lady, a woman of impeccable breeding. How dare he make her want to take that final step on her discoveries of men and have him show her all there was to experience. That was what her betrothed was for.

Arabella's mouth gaped as her gaze followed the taut V of muscle that disappeared into his breeches. She started at her own thoughts, which were anything but innocent. One night when she and Nina had snuck out, they had heard music while passing the mews. They stopped and spied on the servants and what they'd seen there had opened her eyes to what men and women did when alone. Of what the male body looked like in the throes of passion.

She bit her bottom lip, imagining exactly what this captain would look like in such a position.

Arabella started at her own thoughts. What was she doing thinking in such a way? This man had kidnapped her. Made her work like a servant. Forgot to feed her. He'd be lucky if she didn't spit in his face. "I do believe you've forgotten something."

He raised his brow and contemplated her with a glance that she didn't even want to surmise over. "What would that be?"

His deep baritone, slightly slurred with liqueur had an odd twang to it. Similar to those who hailed from Scotland. Arabella frowned. Where was he from before sailing the high seas?

"My dinner. If you haven't noticed in your drunken state, it's near the middle of the night and I'm starving. Now turn about and go fetch me some." He laughed. A great holler that irked even more than being starved. He found this amusing? "I'm not joking, Captain Blackmore."

He rubbed his eyes and beckoned to a man she hadn't seen standing behind him in the shadows. Her mouth watered as the smell of chicken broth and a plate of vegetables and bread was placed before her. Never had food been all-consuming and never had she been more desperate to eat it.

The lout didn't move to release her bonds. Was he planning on teasing her with the meal all night? The thought of such punishment almost brought tears to her eyes. "Unless you're going to feed me yourself, you had better untie me."

"Interesting concept and one I'm only too willing to try." He pulled up a chair before her and picked up the bread. The dough smelt newly cooked and delicious. He tore a little bit off and held it before her lips. Arabella met his gaze over the top of his fingers. It wasn't just food he was offering, but a taste of sin. Something told her, should she take a bite, her life would never be the same.

Her heart pounded as she leaned forward and took the food from his fingers.

Stephen inwardly groaned as her sweet lips opened and she took the piece of bread into her mouth. Thoughts of other things going into the orifice bombarded his mind and his cock twitched. He'd planned on staying away. Of letting her starve for one night.

The woman was trouble and more annoying than he thought she was going to be. The fact she had thrown two mops and a bucket overboard irritated and amused him at the same time. Who did that type of tomfoolery?

He hadn't expected it from a woman of her breeding and yet he liked her spirit.

From all reports, she should be frightened of him. Submissive and demure. Instead, he'd been dealt a harridan who hadn't reached old age. She chewed and closed her eyes, seemingly enjoying the repast. A twinge of guilt pricked his conscience. He'd never been one to starve anyone, least of all a woman, but there was something about this minx that rubbed him the wrong way. Or worse, rubbed him entirely the right way.

He cleared his throat. "Better?"

Her glistening, deep green eyes met his and for a moment he lost himself in their depths. She was an exquisite woman. Her body was one he could spend hours devoted to. A nice pair of breasts he'd watched longingly all day, long, lean legs that would wrap nicely about his waist and beautiful brown locks that cascaded over her delicate shoulders.

"Please tell me you're going to give me more than a sliver of bread."

He grinned at her gumption. What a remarkable spirit. He doubted anyone could break her, and he hoped no one ever did. She was magnificent.

Stephen ladled some soup onto the spoon and held it

against her lips. She moaned as the liquid hit her tongue. The intoxicating sound made him fumble with the cutlery. Desire coursed through him and he adjusted his seat knowing if he made it through the meal without ravishing her, it would be a miracle.

His captive ate every bite of her repast. He leaned back in his chair and watched her. She didn't say anything, no thanks or comments on the meal, just held his gaze with a forthrightness he'd never experienced before. Not with a woman at least.

"You're not scared of me, are you?" he asked at length already knowing what the answer would be.

She scoffed. "Why would I be? I'm worth more to you alive than dead. And since I figure we're headed for London I assume you intend to return me to my family when you've been paid your *supposed* debt."

"Not supposed," he said, interrupting her. "Owed."

"In any case, I'm sure Father and you can come to some sort of agreement without my reputation being sullied."

Stephen nodded. "I'm sure we can." He poured some wine before untying her. She grabbed the goblet and drank deep. He really shouldn't have left her for so long. "Tell me, should you escape this kidnapping reputation in tack, just what are the plans for the determined Miss Hester?" Sadness flickered through her gaze and he wondered at it.

"I'm betrothed. In only a few weeks, I'll be Lady Montague. A countess no less. The marriage is set to take place at his country estate in Shropshire. I consider myself very fortunate to marry a man of good breeding and upstanding values. Some of which are noticeably missing on this boat." Her perfect nose rose in the air with her speech.

"Ship." He smiled at her barb. He should call her Cat.

Her claws were sharp enough. "You wound me." He placed his hand across his chest for emphasis. "Do you believe marriage will make you happy? Will the esteemed Lord Montague make you happy?" Stephen started, wondering why he'd ever want to know the answer to such a question. Miss Hester meant nothing to him.

She frowned, small lines appearing between her brows. Instinctively, Stephen reached out and caressed her frown lines away. Touching her like this, without them having argued first sent liquid heat pouring through his veins. The soft flesh did strange things to his innards, made them tighten with need.

"I hope he will."

Stephen hardly heard the whispered words. He traced her perfectly arched brow before letting his hand drop to his side. Not a freckle spotted her nose, not a blemish anywhere. A true English beauty if ever he'd beheld one. "And if he doesn't?"

Somehow he'd leaned closer. Close enough for her breath to whisper against his cheek. He ran his hand down her neck and across her shoulder, her increased breathing making her breasts push against her gown. He clenched his jaw as desire rushed through him.

She shivered. "There is nothing I can do about it in any case. I will have to be content with what I have."

Content? The delectable Miss Hester deserved much more than content. Her life should be full of passion, adventure, life. No matter what his dealings with her father, she deserved much more than mediocre. He wanted to touch her more, to run his hand across her breast and seduce her to sin. Stephen gritted his teeth and pulled back. Fought with what little there was left of him as a gentleman and not act a cad. "If ever you decide to see what life could be like with a real man, just ask me. I'm more than willing to show you."

The words left his mouth before he could stop them. Around this woman, he lost all sense of control and decorum. Her eyes flared before a blush stole over her cheeks. "I'm sure that won't be necessary. In any case, do you not have a woman at some port, just lying about waiting for her pirate captain to ravish her?"

"Ravish? You do hold me in high regard." Sarcasm laced his tone. He liked a good tumble as well as any other, but he never ravished women. Where was the fun in that? Should a woman lay with him, he liked to receive as well as give pleasure. There was nothing he wanted more than a willing participant in bed sport. "Perhaps you ought to have a taste of my abilities. I promise I won't bite. Much."

For the first time he pulled a grin from her lips and it dazzled him silent. He hadn't thought Miss Hester could get any more handsome. How wrong was he?

"Thank you, but no. I'm sure my future husband will do quite well enough. And you never answered my question."

"What question was that?" He crossed his arms over his chest and leaned back in his chair. The thought of Lord Montague doing any woman justice in bed laughable. From what he'd heard of the fortune hunting popinjay, his tastes leaned more toward his own sex than those of the female kind.

"Is there a special woman in your life? Are you married or have you been?" Was that a tinge of interest in her query?

"You do ask a lot of questions for a captive woman. Why would you think I would answer them in the first place?" Stephen asked, enjoying the banter between them.

For the first time since he'd thrown her delectable derriere over his shoulder, she was speaking to him in a relative normal manner.

"I suppose you don't have to. I was just curious about your life. It's a trait my father has tried to cure me of, but with little success. I am what I am."

Stephen caressed a curl that had fallen over her shoulder. Never in his life had he wanted to kiss a woman so much. She watched him, the question in her eyes asking if he would act on his desires or not. "There is nothing wrong with who you are."

"I don't believe you know me well enough to make such a claim." She pushed his hand away. "Now, if you don't mind I'd like to go to bed."

Stephen stood and held out his hand to assist her up. She stared at him a moment before allowing him to help. Her fingers were cool to the touch and so much smaller than his. "I think it's time for you to commence the task I asked of you when you first arrived."

"What task was that?" She stopped near the bed just as she reached for the covers.

"To help me dress and undress. I require your assistance morning and night." He grinned at the disdain that bled into her features.

"The hell I will. Undress yourself and somewhere else. You're not sleeping in here."

He walked over to her and tipped up her chin. Her lips opened on a gasp or invitation he wasn't sure. And as much as he wanted to take her, taste the sweet essence she possessed, he refrained. "Come, Miss Hester. Surely you do not wish to be tied up again until you succumb to my demand."

The look on her face said more than any words could just what he could do with his demand. What a minx. A refreshing, feisty chit. He could get used to having her about.

She huffed out a breath of annoyance and reached for the buttons on his breeches. "Let me get a couple of things clear before I do this. Under no circumstance do I wish you to think I'm enjoying myself in the least, because I'm not. This is a vile, un-gentlemanly thing to make a woman do under the circumstances."

The first button popped and he swallowed. His body yearned for her. Right at this moment, it wasn't beneath him to beg for just one touch.

"Secondly, should I find out you've gone crowing on deck that you've made your captive demean herself so, I will cut off the appendage you're so determined for me to see and when you least expect it. Do you understand?" Her voice was authoritative, and damn well near undid him. He loved a woman with courage.

"I understand entirely," he said on a gasp when she accidentally grazed said appendage.

She ripped the buttons clear apart. "Very good then. We're in agreement."

❦

The bravado Arabella fought hard to show was exactly that. A show. In no way was she un-rattled by what the captain was making her do. Her fingers trembled as she slipped his breeches over his bottom and down his thighs. She let out a breath when she noted the lack of drawers under his pants.

Worse was the fact she allowed her hand to touch his skin, reveling in the warmth and smoothness begging to be stroked.

She had to bend before him to take them to his feet

and she would swear she heard him groan. She wasn't fool enough not to know he was enjoying himself. He probably wished she would touch him, tease him into seducing her.

Never. There was no chance of that happening, in this lifetime or the next. He may be the most handsome pirate she'd ever seen and possibly the nicest one, other than the tying up and forgetfulness with food, but that didn't change what he'd done to her.

"There, you're naked. Are you happy now?" She raised her brow and tried not to notice the jutting member of his body that demanded attention. Arabella stood, hating the fact that once again the captain smelled of the sea, with a hint of brandy. His hands clenched at his side and she tore her gaze away from his body to look him in the eye. "Well?" she asked at length when he didn't reply.

"You're determined to ignore me, aren't you?" He stroked himself and Arabella didn't know where to look or what to do.

She walked around him not wanting him to see her mouth agape like a fish. She fiddled with the bed sheets. "Determined? I thought I *was* ignoring you." Sitting on the bed, she removed her slippers and slid off her stockings. It was so lovely not having shoes on after so many days, but what she'd really love was a bath. A nice, deep, fragrant bath.

Laying on the bed, she turned away and set herself to going to sleep. It was little use. As soon as she closed her eyes, images of his form bombarded her mind. Long, muscular thighs. An abdomen she could use to wash clothing on. Eyes that were sleepy with sin and need. His member...

Arabella's stomach clenched. She shouldn't even be thinking of him in those terms. Her body was becoming a traitor. The captain was a criminal, and awful blot on society that no woman of her class would ever look at or give themselves to. Maybe the trauma of being kidnapped had damaged her mind and principles in some way.

The bed dipped and her tension spiked. Whether in fear or trepidation she wasn't sure. Without another word the captain settled into the bedding, seemingly content to sleep without molesting her. It was a ridiculous situation. Making out one was asleep when you knew the other was not was absurd.

She peeked at him through her lashes. He was lying on his back, one arm acting as a pillow beneath his head. He stared at the ceiling, his face relaxed but contemplative. What was he thinking? Was he hoping she'd crawl up over his chest and kiss him? Slide her hand along his smooth stomach until she hit the apex between his thighs and stroked him harder than he already was. Heat pooled at her core and she inwardly cursed herself to Hades.

"Goodnight, Arabella."

The air in her lungs vanished. Her name on his lips wasn't anything she wished to hear now or ever. It rolled off his tongue in the brogue she'd heard only once before, eliciting a deep-rooted sense of rightness to spark in her soul.

Damn the man. "Go to hell," she replied, rolling over once more and giving him the view of her back.

Her conflicting emotions were absurd as the situation she now found herself. Arabella clutched the pillow, refusing her body to turn back to the captain and take what he offered. A night of passion, most likely the only one she'd ever enjoy, but she could not. He had wronged her, taken her against her will, damn it. In Malta her life had been organized, planned, her future set and no matter how droll it would be, it was her lot in life. She could not go to her marriage bed ruined.

Despair washed over her like a wave. Who was she kidding. She was already ruined thanks to the ass beside her. Damn him.

CHAPTER 4

Arabella woke in a tangle of arms and legs. A solid heartbeat thumped beneath her cheek and she stilled as realization hit her. She could not be asleep, cuddled up to the most inappropriate man she'd ever met in her entire life.

His hand slid down her back and she inwardly cursed. The shift she'd worn to bed had twisted about her waist and she couldn't move. She tried to ease away, not wanting him to find her in his arms like some wanton hussy he picked up in a port.

"Going somewhere?" His voice sounded husky with sleep.

Arabella jumped and met his gaze. "I think it's obvious that I am." She scrambled back, but not quick enough. He rolled her onto her back, his lower body tantalizingly close to the apex of her thighs. Again, heat pooled at her core and she fought not to let her legs open to him and show him without words what her body desperately craved.

The touch of a man. Not a boy who ignored her, enjoyed his friends more than his betrothed, but a man who enjoyed women, pleasured them and left them wanting more.

As if sensing her need he pushed gently against her. Arabella gasped and fought not to give way to him. He no longer looked sleepy but intense. His whole being zeroed in on her, waiting, wanting, asking a silent question she could not answer.

Not because she didn't want to but because her voice seemed incapable of function. She cleared her throat. "Get off, you brute."

He did as she asked, grinning before he sat up on his elbow. The sheet dipped past his stomach and again she was reminded of his spectacular form. He patted the bed. "I was enjoying our closer arrangement. Perhaps you'd like to remove your shift and come and join me again."

Arabella clenched her fists. He was impossible. *Impossible to ignore...* "I think somewhere along our association you've become confused. I don't want to have anything to do with you. I just want you to get whatever you think is owed so I can leave. This is all."

"Did you know that when you slept in my arms, you stroked my chest and sighed? I think deep down in your conscience you want me." *Could he sound more smug?* He flipped the bedding back and stood, giving her the first full view of his back.

Oh, good God. It was perhaps just as perfect as his front. She shook her head as he stretched, even at this distance, his strength and height making her feel minuscule in the room.

"That's it. I've had enough." Arabella pulled at her skirts that were caught beneath her bottom; fell onto the floor trying to get as far away as possible from him that she could. She scrambled to her feet, stormed over to his armoire and pulled out a shirt and breeches. Walking up to him she threw them at his face. "I demand you clothe yourself immediately."

"Not without the help of my new valet."

A lock of hair slipped over his brow as he drew the clothing away from his face. He was a fiend of the worst kind. She had to give it to him, he really was trying to annoy her to the point of despair. Arabella laughed despite herself. "You're impossible."

He pulled the shirt on himself and grinned. "And you, miss, look delightful when you laugh. You should do it more often. It may delay the effects of becoming an ape leader before your time."

She gasped as he strode out the room, naked from the waist down and without a care to the fact. He was an enigma and one she doubted she would ever understand.

Arabella paced the small chamber, the temper boiling inside her hotter than the Italian sun. For two days she'd been locked up in the room with minimal interaction with people. At this moment in time, she'd gladly talk to the lowest deckhand if only to hear someone else's voice.

She slumped onto a chair. Why had she been left alone again. They had parted on reasonable terms. Other than her being called a future ape leader, but then she really couldn't see the insult in that. There were worst things.

Over the last few days she had thought about putting her circumstances aside, and forming a truce. She couldn't stay indoors forever. Just a day was enough to put her into a decline. It couldn't go on.

The door opened and four men entered. Arabella clutched the desk chair she was sitting on not fully comprehending why they were there until they pulled a tub through the door and placed it to one the side of the room.

Over the next few minutes, other men brought in buckets of steaming water.

A bath. There was a god.

"Forgive me for leaving you to your own devices for the last two days. I was required on deck." The captain walked over to a shelf and grabbed what she assumed to be soap. "You may bathe in privacy. Come outside when you're done. I wish to wash also. You'll find clean clothes that may possibly fit you in the chest of drawers, although you'll have to be content with men's clothing. It's all I have."

Arabella nodded. "Thank you. I can't tell you enough how much I want a bath." Just the thought of that warm soapy water made her want to strip down to nothing right now. Captain present or not.

No sooner had he arrived he was gone again. She undressed quickly and moaned as she slid into the fresh, hot water. She washed herself thoroughly, scrubbed her hair and then laid back to soak for a few minutes. Days of grime became nothing but a memory as the water cleaned away her immediate troubles.

Should she die right now she'd die happy.

※

Stephen looked over to his cabin door once more and still Arabella wasn't to be seen. It had been well half an hour since he'd left her to bathe. Surely, the woman wouldn't still be in there.

The thought of the soapy water cleansing her skin made him ache. He ran a hand through his hair before turning about and heading toward his room. Maybe she'd fallen asleep. Drowned even. Was right at this moment dead. He quickened his pace, and without heed he threw open the cabin door and stopped.

His imagination had nothing on what Arabella looked like, naked, dripping with water and smelling of lavender. She squealed and pulled the small drying towel about her, but it didn't matter. The image of her long legs, perfectly sculptured waist and breasts that would fit his hands nicely burned permanently into his mind.

"What do you think you're doing? Get out."

A blush stole up her neck making her cheeks very pink. "You were taking so long. I thought you may have fallen asleep and drowned."

She rolled her eyes. "I'm not a child. Don't be absurd."

"I can see that," he stated, allowing his gaze to slide over her again. His jaw clenched. Shutting the door behind him, he leaned against the wood. Hoped that in some minuscule way it would keep him from striding over to her and kissing her senseless.

Her eyes narrowed. "You shouldn't be staring at me like that and you shouldn't be in this room. You need to leave so I can dress."

Stephen grunted. He supposed he should do everything she asked, but he could not. "If I do as you ask I want a favor in return."

"What sort of favor?" She stepped back, wariness settling in her eyes, but Stephen could also see curiosity mingled within her dark green orbs.

"Come here." His command surprisingly worked. Each step she took swayed her hips in a silent seduction. As she stood before him, he ran his gaze over her delicate features. She was exquisite and not someone who should be wasted on Lord Montague. That man couldn't appreciate the woman's form if she was laid out before him on a salver.

He ran a finger down her arm and tiny goosebumps rose on her skin. "Have you ever been kissed?"

She didn't reply, only shook her head.

"Then let me remedy that immediately." Stephen leaned down, cupped her jaw and claimed her lips. Kissed her with all the pent up passion, desire, and respect he could summon.

Her lips were soft and he couldn't help but notice untutored. He supped from them, beckoned her to copy, to follow his lead. And just as quick as her wit, Arabella kissed him back. He groaned as her fingers spiked into his hair, pulling him close. Fire coursed through his blood and he walked her backwards before pushing her up against the door.

Her mouth opened on a whimper and without thought, he took advantage and deepened the embrace. She tasted of wine and smelt of flowers. An intoxicating mix if ever there was one. The glide of their mouths, wet and wanton made him burn. With a will of their own, his hands ventured from her jaw to travel down her waist.

Arabella wrapped her arms about his neck and took control of the kiss. For a moment, Stephen lost all thought as her towel slipped to the floor. He grappled with the fact she was naked in his arms, and seemingly oblivious to what had happened to her only piece of modesty. For a woman who was new to the art of kissing, she was doing a wonderful job.

Her breasts pushed against his chest, her nipples hard little beads that begged to be kissed. There was no doubt where this kiss was leading, and Stephen wanted to conclude this little interlude with his cock buried deep in her willing core. He clasped the perfect mounds of her ass and the action shocked the little minx to her senses. *Clever lass.* Had she kept kissing him the way she was he would've seen just how far she would've taken the interlude.

She squeaked, her eyes darting down to her naked form before she pushed at his chest. With reluctance, he pulled back, giving her the space she wanted. Her emerald eyes sparkled with desire and now unfortunately, loathing. His gut clenched. Touché, Arabella for he too wanted her more than he'd wanted any other woman before, and yet his loathing was not the same as hers.

He loathed the fact she was the daughter of a man who had wronged him. Loathed that his grandfather, his excess in the gambling hells had made it impossible for Stephen to court her as an equal, as it should have been.

"Excuse me." She walked over to his cupboard and pulled out some clothes. Without a flicker of embarrassment, she dressed before him. Stephen stood rooted on the spot, his mouth gaped and his body ached with longing and denial. Of all things holy he wanted her.

He also knew when to stay away. She walked out and slammed the door behind her. She was angry with him and with herself, he could guess. He ran his hands through his hair. He shouldn't have kissed her. She wasn't here to become his chère-amie no matter how much he wanted the fact.

Needing to distract himself, he quickly stripped and jumped into the tepid bath water. It didn't help him. If anything, the aroma wafting up only pulled him further into the delectable lady's lures.

He ran a hand over his jaw and scratched the stubble there. He wanted to have her, that was a given. But this endless longing to hold her, tease her, talk to the chit was beyond his normal reactions when around a beautiful woman.

So why was it so different with Arabella?

The fact she hated him, wanted nothing to do with him and certainly had no desire to bed him couldn't possibly be the reason. Although after their last interaction, the latter may not be so true. Did she desire him as well? The thought jumbled in his mind and even Stephen had a hard time disbelieving it.

Someone so unattainable, above him, beyond his social sphere shouldn't be someone he wanted so much.

But he did. Desperately.

He found Arabella at the bow looking out at the setting sun. The light altered the color of her hair and sent strands of fire flicking throughout the dark brown locks. "You may dine on the deck with me and my crew tonight."

She didn't acknowledge him; just continued to stare straight ahead. "You can't kiss me like that again." Arabella turned and pinned him with her determined gaze. "I'm betrothed. You're a kidnapping pirate. You cannot go about kissing women you're only too happy to steal away and ruin. I won't allow it."

The mention of her future husband made his gut churn like he'd eaten rotten fish. "Are you in any way acquainted with Lord Montague? Or was this just another absurd notion of your father's?"

"Don't mention my father to me. You're already reprehensible, don't make yourself irredeemable," she said, her voice thrumming with anger.

Stephen stepped before her and clasped her arm, stopping her from escaping. "Does that mean you think me redeemable?" He grinned at her ferocious glare. "That the impeccable Miss Hester could possibly look past my misdemeanors and see the man inside." Stephen started at his own words. Did he even want her to see the real him? And if she did, what was he willing to do about that.

Arabella burst out laughing and he raised his brow. He thought over what he'd said and couldn't see anything amusing in it whatsoever. "Are you finished?" he asked at length, when tears threatened to spill down her cheeks.

"The man inside? You'll be sprouting poetry next,

Captain Blackmore." She poked him in the chest and his body reveled in the contact. Little as it was. "I will never see you as anything other than a lying, stealing rogue. I should think you made the decision to be who you are many years ago, and set out quite determinedly to accomplish it. And since being here this last week or so, I see nothing but amusement and enjoyment with how your life has played out. There is no underlying man inside. Only an ass."

Stephen swallowed the bile that rose in his throat. The venom in which she'd spoken only proved that she believed every word she said. Yes, he'd had to choose a certain way of life, and maybe it wasn't what he should've been born to do, but it was the only option open to him. The fact that her father now owed him funds that were imperative to secure his and his men's future only coiled the anger inside him tighter.

He was asset rich, but coin poor and the repairs required to his estate were substantial. Once his life on the high seas was over, he'd planned on living in Scotland and enjoying the rest of his days in peace and above the law. Arabella's father and his lack of payment had already delayed him by a year. Everything cost something, and it was about time Lord Hester came to realize that fact.

He gritted his teeth. "Well, my dear. I look forward to proving you wrong."

She patted his chest, the gesture patronizing. "Don't tax yourself. It's not possible." She walked over to the makeshift table on which dinner was being laid out and sat.

He would look forward to the challenge.

CHAPTER 5

Arabella spooned up the fish soup, a soup that would've tasted nice should it not contain fish. She tried to hide her shudder of revulsion and failed. How people could live months on end, day after day of this type of diet baffled her.

The stars were out this fine night, not a cloud to be seen and it was as if she could reach out and hand and pick one from the sky. The water lapped at the ship's side as it forced its way through the waves. It was truly beautiful. She adjusted her seat and enjoyed the freedom of movement her breeches afforded her. How wonderful it must be for men, to be able to wear such clothing always.

But it was all a rouse, for sitting at their table was their captive. A woman here against her will and they all knew it. Picking up a dried piece of bread, she broke it in two and took a bite, watching the captain as he spoke to his crew at the opposite end.

His hair was ruffled, his shirt partly open and exposing the light dusting of hair that feathered his chest. One arm lay lazily before him on the table, while the other was slumped over the back of his chair. She shook her head. It wasn't a pose she was used to seeing at table. No one ever sat so relaxed, certainly not in her world. The captain threw back his head and laughed and Arabella had to admit, she enjoyed this ease of speech and meal more than the one she grew up having.

She turned to the man sitting beside her. "How long will it be before we make England?"

He choked on his brew and punched his chest to clear his airways. "It's a six-week trip, miss. I should think we'll not see London for another four and a bit weeks yet."

Arabella nodded having figured the same. "Will the captain not stop for supplies along the way?" If they docked, she could try to escape. It was worth the risk. The captain joked with one of the deckhands and drew her attention to his lovely mouth. A mouth that had kissed her beyond thought only hours earlier, leaving her with emotions so conflicting she'd not known what to say or how to react ever since.

Without thought she licked her lips just as he caught her eye. His mouth lifted into a knowing grin and her palms started to sweat. She shouldn't be attracted to him and had in fact protested to the very infuriating man that she never would be. But she was. Never had she found a man more attractive in her life. The reflection infuriated her as much as it excited her.

She was on a ship, in the middle of the Mediterranean, could she throw caution aside and do what she wanted for the first time in her life? Such actions went against everything she'd been brought up to believe, to think and act, but what was life without a little adventure or so others had said.

Of course, it would mean she would have to tell the captain she wanted adventure, to live free until the time came that she was returned to her father, especially if she wanted him to kiss her again. Or maybe she'd just let him try and seduce her and let him think it was entirely his idea. Such a ploy would certainly save her pride, and yet, could she wait so long for him to kiss her again?

What a fool she was. Had she not just argued with him that she would never allow him to kiss her again? And here she was, with a little wine in her belly, moonlit night and a handsome captain at the end of a dinner table and she'd succumbed to the romance of it all.

Arabella let her gaze travel over his form and noted his hand was fisted on the table. She caught his heated, intense gaze and held it. What she was contemplating was wrong, scandalous in fact and ruining. Should she be caught, her good social standing would be a thing of the past. Her betrothed would turn away from her in disgrace.

Not that the former would bother her much. Lord Montague hadn't taken much interest in her even after the notices were posted about their forthcoming nuptials. Too interested in his friends and the enjoyment of the island life that he could experience. But Captain Blackmore was interested. And by the hooded, lazy gaze as he took his fill of her, his seduction of her would be whenever she allowed it.

The sound of her dinner companion's voice jolted her back. "The captain has enough supplies to last us until we reach England. No point trying to escape, miss. You're as stuck here on this ship as much as the rest of us."

Arabella nodded. "I thought as much." She turned toward the deckhand. "Have you ever kidnapped a woman before or am I the only lucky one?"

He laughed. "We're not even really pirates. We ship contraband, smuggle sometimes into England when toffs like you require goods. The cargo has always been menial fare that wouldn't hurt a fly. So when the captain discussed taking you onboard against yer will we were all very against the idea. But the funds that are due to the captain will enable him to leave for Scotland and his crew to start a fresh life wherever we want. 'Tis only fair the amount is paid."

"And you too believe that my father owes this money?" She thought back on her papa and his penchant for gambling. It wouldn't surprise her in the least that he'd smuggled goods into England to make a profit, whether it was against the English law or not. Where there was quick blunt to be made, her father normally sniffed it out like a beagle. But to not pay a debt seemed to go against the character she thought she knew so well.

"He does. I just hope for your sake he can pay it. The men here never wanted to pull you into this mess, but the captain having seen you one day wouldn't hear sense. It was as if he—"

"Miss Hester, it's time you went back to the cabin." The captain cut into the deckhand's speech and left Arabella grappling to know what he was going to say.

"I'm not ready to go below decks. I'm having a lovely conversation with Mr...?"

The deckhand grinned. "Call me Joe."

"I'm having a lovely conversation with Joe. You retire if you wish, but I'm staying here." Arabella took a sip of wine and squealed, dropping the beverage over the table when the captain picked her up, threw her over his shoulder and started to storm toward the cabin's door. She clasped his back and realized her mistake as soon as she felt the corded muscles that ran down his spine.

The warmth of his skin penetrated his shirt, and her stomach tied into knots. He was so strong, virile that it was overwhelming. She didn't say anything else. Instead, she waited for him to place her back onto her feet so she could look at him in the eye when she gave him a proper set down.

"How dare you treat me like a piece of meat? It has been many years since I've been made to go to bed like an errant child. I may not be a Duke's daughter, but I am a well-bred, respectable woman. Does that mean anything to you?'

"I know exactly who you are." His words were low with a savage edge and the pent up desire she read in his gaze sent her heart to pound. *He was going to kiss her…*

Arabella gasped as he took her lips, using her shock to deepen the embrace. This was madness. An addictive disease that no matter how destructive, one she didn't wish to be cured of.

He nipped her lips, suckled the bottom one before pulling away. Her body wanted to melt into a puddle at his feet. Instead, she grasped his shirt and wouldn't allow the distance to go any further. "And who is that?"

He clasped the collar of her shirt and slipped it off her shoulder, revealing a good portion of skin. "The woman I want in my bed, tonight and for as many nights to come for as long as she'll allow it."

"You know what you're asking of me." Arabella cleared her throat, even to her, her voice sounded husky and nothing like the forthright, determined voice she usually sported.

His eyes darkened in determination. "I do. And yet I'm still going to ask."

He swung her into his arms and carried her over to the bed. Could she actually do this? Throw her virginity away and possibly her future? He nuzzled her neck, his breath sending delicious shivers down her skin.

Oh yes, she could throw it all away if only he kept making her feel like this.

Special, needy and expectant, like she was the only woman in the world.

The captain clasped the hem of her shirt and ripped it off. Arabella sank into the bedding and watched enthralled as he came down over her before she realized something imperative. "Somehow this seems wrong when I don't know your first name."

He clutched her waist and idly ran a finger over her stomach. "My name's Stephen."

Stephen... It suited him. He unclasped the buttons on her buckskin breeches before touching her where no one had ever touched before. Arabella closed her eyes and reveled in the delicious friction he created against her flesh. Fire burned through her blood, a delicious ache settled between her legs and she moaned as fingers delved within her. Unable to stem her need, she lifted against his hand, wanting more of his touch.

His rumbling chuckle against her lips tickled. "You like that, do you not?" His touch shifted to her most intimate of places she gasped.

"Very much so. Tell me what you're doing to me."

"I'm kissing you. Letting you feel with my tongue, with my lips." He took her mouth in a searing kiss, dragging her further into a world she'd often wondered about, but was forever elusive. "How much I want to take you and make you mine."

Arabella slid her hand under his shirt and pulled it out of his breeches, dragging it over his head. The muscles of his shoulders flexed, his pectoral and abdomen rippled with the movement. Her mouth dried.

Magnificent.

Taking a chance, she kissed her way down his chest,

before teasing a nipple with her tongue. She heard his intake of breath and stopped. "Have I hurt you?"

He pulled away, kneeling between her thighs. "Not in the way you think."

Arabella laughed as he ripped her breeches down her legs and threw them absently to the floor. His intense gaze branded her as his as he settled back over her. His hard member pushed against her mons, rubbed along her slickened heat. The friction from the soft yet rigid appendage did odd things to her insides. Her stomach twisted in delicious knots. "Yes. Keep doing that."

The tip of his member entered her and she slipped her legs up around his waist.

"You make me so desperate I can scarcely breathe."

Arabella bit her lip, loving that she could make him lose a little control. His breath was ragged and she undulated beneath him, wanting more, needing Stephen to make her his. "Is this what I'm supposed to do?" He pushed a little further in and a slight sting dampened her desire.

He nodded, rolling his hips a little as he pushed some more. "It's very good. Too good," he said, before thrusting once and taking her fully.

Arabella froze as the width and length of him wasn't what she'd expected. Deep inside, she felt full, sore, but also impatient to see what else he could do for her. She wanted to experience it all, and now wasn't soon enough.

"I'm sorry." He kissed her, swooped her into a void of need before slowly, with each thrust of tongue, matched the stroke with his hips. "I didn't want to hurt you."

The sincerity in his voice made her heart thump. "I'm well." She wrapped her arms about his neck and smiled. "Please proceed."

Stephen chuckled, but took each stroke slowly. He was large, probably too large for a virgin of her petite frame. But women like Arabella were rare and the thought of her future husband taking her in such a way, consummating their marriage wasn't to be borne.

The fop she was betrothed to wouldn't be gentle. Why, he'd more likely turn her over and sodomise her instead.

She undulated beneath him, her breasts rocking with their lovemaking, and he felt sure his choice to have her was right. Maybe not morally right, but for Arabella he'd done her a favor in showing her what it was supposed to be like for a woman when laying with a man.

Heat, the slap of skin on skin, moistness and moans were what was supposed to be heard and felt when a woman was in the throes of passion. Not silence, whimpering like he instinctively knew she would endure with Lord Montague.

"Have you ever found bliss, Arabella?"

She opened her eyes and he lost a part of himself to their crystalline beauty. "What is that? I've seen women with men before and they seem to enjoy it, but I've never done anything like this before."

"The fact that you do not know is all the answer I need." He rolled onto his back and pulled her to straddle his waist. He'd not thought she could be any more beautiful, but above, him, in control of their enjoyment, she was magnificent.

She braced herself on top of him, her hands idly feeling the hair on his chest. "Is this position even possible?"

"Absolutely. Just lift yourself as if you're riding a horse, but bring yourself down on me. Nice and slowly, but continuously. I promise you'll enjoy it." He clasped her hips and helped her, as the first few movements were awkward. It didn't take her long before she'd mastered the sexual position.

Stephen bit the inside of his lip as she rode him, her hips swaying slightly that matched her bountiful breasts. He shut his eyes not needing to see the stimulating picture she made. He wouldn't come until she'd found her own pleasure, and by the increased pants and slickness between them, it wouldn't be long.

A self-satisfied smile tweaked his lips knowing she was enjoying this as much as he.

"Yes, keep doing that." Oh God, she was going to kill him. Her body, tight and willing drew him along, pulled at his cock and made him want to blow between her legs. How did she learn so quickly? "Ride me until you come. Use me."

The sight of her fondling her own breast was too much. Stephen swore. He couldn't take much more. She rode him, her strokes consistent and mind numbing.

Stephen grabbed her hips, helped her to come down hard with each stroke. Her gaze went hazy with awe. "Is that good?" he panted, knowing it felt bloody fantastic.

"Yes," she gasped. "Oh yes it is."

Their speed increased. The sound of skin slapping skin echoed throughout the space along with the scent of sex and still he urged her on, wanting to see her shatter for the very first time in his arms. It didn't take long.

Arabella moaned, her head flopping back as she rode him through her release. Stephen, leaving one hand on her hips, clasped her breast and tweaked a pinkened, erect nipple. She gasped again, her body convulsing around his cock and dragging him along to join her.

Lights blazed behind his eyes as his body released days

of pent up desire. He took her without heed or care, allowed them both to come apart within each other's arms.

Arabella collapsed beside him, both their breathing ragged. Not willing to let her scoot away, he pulled her into the nook of his shoulder to keep her close.

"I'm…speechless," she said, sighing and sounding sleepy.

Stephen laughed. She was more than speechless. She was thoroughly ruined and by him. Never had he felt more like a cad or like someone who'd given a precious gift to a woman who otherwise may have never known the pleasure that could be had between two people. "And now you know."

She looked up at him and the trust he read in her gaze unsettled him a little. "What?"

"What pleasure is." He grinned at the blush that stole over her cheeks. How after what they'd just done she could be embarrassed he had no clue. "I gather you rather enjoyed it."

Arabella grinned and started to play with his chest hair. "I did. Rather a lot, I'm afraid. Which could be a bad thing."

"How so?" He didn't think such a thing could ever be bad, especially if he had her before him, opening for him, beckoning him with her gaze. His cock twitched at the thought.

"Because I'll want to do it again." She held his gaze, not an ounce of fear in her declaration.

Relief poured through him that he'd not scared her off. "Well, I'm never one to disappoint a lady."

She raised her brow and threw him a knowing grin. "Not with sex it would seem."

"Touché. Not with sex at least." He laughed, rolling her onto his back and taking her again. With each kiss, each embrace or touch they shared, Stephen felt his life changing, growing brighter, clearer than ever before. Arabella was delightful, a willing companion in his bed, laughed and took charge when she wanted. She was a breath of fresh air in a life that had stagnated a long time ago.

CHAPTER 6

The next few weeks passed in a haze of desire, stolen moments and laughter.

Arabella couldn't remember when she'd had a more delightful time in her life. Somehow, Stephen brought out the best in her in what could possibly be the worst time of her life. Which was interesting since he was the root of her problems or at least, part of them.

Stephen changed his mind as to their destination and had sailed past the entrance to the Thames river and had instead, continued along the English coast toward Cornwall. Today they were anchoring off a remote cove where a small village could be seen scattered back from the land behind. A magnificent house further up the coast looked over the township and rocky outcrop that made up part of the coast. She stood beside the wheel and watched the men go about their jobs. They were so close to home. It had been months since she'd set foot on English soil.

Arabella frowned, not knowing how seeing England again made her feel. She supposed a little sad that her voyage with Stephen was ending. That soon he would hand her over to her father once the debt was paid, and her betrothed if he would still have her, which she hoped he would not. The thought of laying with another man other than Stephen made her stomach roil in dread.

Lord Montague and their impending marriage floated through her mind. Did he know of her disappearance? Had her father somehow managed word to him and even now, were both in pursuit to rescue her? She scoffed, doubting his lordship cared a fig what happened to her person. His only concern would be for the money he'd lose in not marrying her.

She bit her lip to stop her eyes from welling up. The thought of being removed from Stephen's side and embarking on a life she had promised another left her hollow. She didn't even know Lord Montague. Had hardly spent any time being acquainted when he was in Malta with her family. The image of laying under him, making love as a wife should with her husband brought revulsion coursing through her blood. If she were lucky, his lordship would not want someone who is sullied, would look elsewhere for a wife. Such hope didn't last long, not when her marriage portion was large enough to forgive any misdemeanor by her.

Footsteps sounded behind her and she knew by the fall of the boot who it was without turning. Strong arms encircled her waist and she settled against his chest the fresh smell of the ocean and soap coming with him. "Do you wish to join me on the mainland? It may be nice for you to be on land for a little while."

"I would love to." She turned and pushed the lock of hair out of his face. A few of the crew smiled in their direction, some making light of the captain's public show of affection. Arabella reveled in it, loving how he had no qualms in kissing or touching her anywhere on the ship and before anyone. "How long do you think your business will take?"

"A day or so. No more." He walked her backward and the cool wood of the railing sat against her back. "Why? Impatient to get me back in our cabin?"

She slapped his chest but undulated against his hardness, loving the fact he now called his quarters *their* quarters. "Of course not. Whatever gave you that impression?" He laughed and shook his head. Over the last few weeks, a closeness had formed between them. One that she'd not thought possible, especially with how they were thrown together in the first place. With Stephen by her side, Arabella felt free, more herself than any other time she can remember. There were no rules with him, no must and must not's in life.

"You have a certain look in your eye, one where I believe you'd like nothing more than to take me somewhere private and do wickedly naughty things to me," he grinned, a devilish light in his eyes.

"No I do not. You're simply imagining things. Now come, we're getting closer to the coast and I need to change into appropriate clothing for a woman." Not that she'd like to change out of her breeches, loose fitting shirt and jacket. Never had she ever been so comfortable in clothing in her life. The fact she could get about with ease and with little fuss was liberating.

"Of course. Lead the way, my dear. Any excuse helping you change."

Arabella laughed. "You're incorrigible." But she pulled him along with her in any case.

. . .

They anchored late in the afternoon, just as the sun started to disappear behind darkened clouds to the west. It was only a short boat journey to the quaint town. Thatched roofed homes and walls that were made of wood and plaster ran along the foreshore a little back from the beach. Children scooted about playing, some people walked along the cobbled streets entering a few stores that sold particular goods. A highly polished carriage was being unhitched and unloaded at the Boar and Hound Inn. It was a lovely location, very English and welcoming.

Arabella followed Stephen up a side street off the main thoroughfare and was surprised to see an old woman standing on the street beside a cottage door smiling at them. He jogged toward her and picked up the lady and spun her about, laughing. Arabella stopped and just watched. From the love and jovial exclamations the woman was making, she gathered his important business was seeing his mother or some relative.

Stephen gestured for her to join them, and her heart squeezed that he would include her in this. The older woman was a lovely lady, very welcoming and happy to see her son. Introductions were performed and they took afternoon tea with his mother. Arabella considered the lady's perfect manners and impeccable speech which seemed at odds to her sons employment. Again she wondered who Stephen really was and what his history had been. Something told her he wasn't only just a pirate.

They weren't able to stay long much to her surprise. Stephen had other business at the inn, but he promised his mother he would visit again and discuss all that was necessary then. Arabella bid farewell, but was unsure as to what Stephen had meant. What was necessary with his life and what did it have to do with his mother?

A short time later, they walked into the taproom of the inn. Arabella looked about while Stephen organized a private dining chamber. The room was dim, with a burning fire that sat directly across from the bar. Stephen threw orders about like a seasoned gentleman of the *ton*, and once more Arabella was struck by how commanding, autocratic he was. Their weeks together had brought them close in every sense except in the one way that mattered most to her. Who was this man? What had happened in his past that he now sailed the high seas for a living?

He was still a mystery. She knew nothing of his past, of his life outside the captioning the ship or what he'd like to do in the future. And today with his mother only confirmed her suspicions he was hiding something.

But what? And why?

The innkeeper, an elderly, rotund man led them off into a little room that had a roaring fire and a beautiful view of the seaside beyond.

Small vessels dotted the shallow coastal water and Arabella stepped over toward the fire to warm herself. Stephen sank with a sigh into a settee and shut his eyes. The storm that had been on the horizon earlier in the day was starting to show its presence as the wind picked up and rain started to spatter against the windowpane.

"You said you have other business here. Are you meeting someone else?"

Stephen ran a hand through his hair making it stand on end. He cocked one eye open. "I am. Yes. He should be here after dinner, which should be served soon." He gestured to the seat beside him. "Come. Sit with me."

Arabella sat, not liking how he seemed a little ill at ease. "Is something troubling you?"

He pulled out a missive and passed it to her. It was

from Lord Montague. She started for a moment before tearing the missive open.

Captain,

I'm shocked that you would steal away the woman who is to become my wife in only a few weeks' time. I should imagine if you're reading this missive you should also be looking over your shoulder as I'm going to have my revenge on you.

If one hair is misplaced on Miss Hester's head I shall have great enjoyment hurting you in any torturous way possible. It is well advised that the moment you make land in England you hand over my betrothed immediately if I'm not there to make you do so. Not that by doing so will alter the course of your future. You will hang for this crime, you dirty pirate scum.

That is one promise I will make and hold true.

Lord Montague.

Arabella screwed up the letter and threw it into the fire. Fear spiked through her at being ripped away from the one man she'd ever cared for. To be placed with peer who held her in little regard other than monetary value.

Stephen didn't say anything, just watched her as she fiddled with her skirts. "I suppose we should discuss what you're planning to do with me and when you're going to be rid of me as well."

"And if I don't want to be rid of you. What then?" He turned and met her gaze fully, his eyes as bleak as her own emotions. "Will you leave me anyway, Arabella?"

She stood, needing space. "You know I cannot stay. They will kill you if they ever caught you. The banns have been called, here and in Malta. Everyone knows I'm to marry Lord Montague. You seek revenge on my father, you're using me for leverage to gain payment. That fact is not something to be passed over and ignored."

"I know that." He stood, towering over her and her body yearned to lean into him, wrap her arms about his neck and kiss them both senseless. To kiss their problems into oblivion. "Perhaps knowing what your father owes me for will make things clearer for you."

"Please. Enlighten me." She crossed her arms over her chest needing any defense she could gather just in case what Stephen told her was devastating. Just one look at Stephen pulled her into a world that wasn't where she belonged. He was impossible to ignore.

"I'm a smuggler by trade, have been since the man you're about to meet after dinner gifted me his ship. Your father sought me out and asked me to smuggle into England a large shipment of silk to be sold in the markets of London. I should imagine most of the upper ten-thousand are wearing what your father shipped illegally into this country using my men and my ship. The payment due was to be the last monetary amount needed to give them and their families a comfortable life. Better than anything they've ever dreamed of. Your father has stolen this from them and I'm not going to allow that to happen."

Arabella sat back down. "I don't understand. Father has money so why he's refused to pay what was due, illegal or otherwise doesn't make sense. How much is the debt?"

A muscle worked in Stephen's jaw and trepidation settled like a rock in her gut. "Two thousand pounds."

"But he has that." Doesn't he? Of late they had been having food that was less extravagant than usual. Come to think of it, less servants and only one carriage to support their household in Malta. Was her father short of blunt? Were they poor? She swallowed.

"Apparently not," he said.

"What will you do if he cannot pay?" Would he ruin her publicly? Throw her overboard as a waste of his effort and time? She shook the silly thought aside, her mind going places that were less than helpful. At times such as these one needed a clear mind, free to think rationally.

"I will ruin him." *And you as well.* The unspoken words hung between them like a noose.

She clasped his hand. "Perhaps if I speak to my father I can get him to pay you and there be no need for any further trouble." Although the more Arabella thought about the strictures of her life of late, something told her that her father wasn't going to be able to pay no matter how much she wished it.

A knock sounded at the door before a tall man, dressed in attire Arabella had only ever seen in the highest ranks of society. In her shabby dress, stained and torn in parts it left her feeling inadequate and poor. She checked her gown, pleating a section of her skirt to try and hide the small tear.

The gentleman's eyes widened when he spotted her, but he continued into the room and greeted Stephen with warmth. Who was he?

"And who is this?" the man asked, nodding toward her.

Arabella frowned, not liking how this gentleman's tone lacked warmth when speaking of her.

"This is Miss Arabella Hester. Sir Ronald Hester's daughter." Stephen turned to her. "Arabella, this is Gabriel Lyons, the Duke of Dale."

She felt her mouth fall open and she nodded in hello. How was it Stephen knew a duke?

"*Miss* Arabella, is it?" The word was accentuated and had it been as sharp like a knife, she didn't hesitate to think Stephen would've been cut. "As in unmarried and from looking about this room and seeing no maid I can assume, unchaperoned…" The duke sighed. "I had hoped the rumors were false."

For the first time since she'd known Stephen he looked sheepish. "Dinner is about to be served. We'll discuss this later. Alone."

The gentlemen glared at each other and Arabella sat down at the wooden table as dinner was brought in by two kitchen girls. Night was falling and the storm howled outside. Candles were brought in and the fire stoked to ward off the dark chill of the night. The windows whistled, a cold draft running down her spine and making her flimsy gown less than ideal in such weather. She shivered, wishing she had a shawl or blanket.

"We'll be staying here for the night," Stephen said, as if sensing her unvoiced concern. He joined her at the table, but didn't meet her eye. The other gentleman did the same and a quiet awkwardness settled around them. The duke did not try and hide his disappointment at seeing her here. She quickly ate the stew and welcomed the maid who came in to take her upstairs. Bidding the men goodnight, she left them to their discussions.

◈

"What the hell is going on? Rumors reached me in London over your escapades or should I say your kidnapping of innocent women. What are you doing?" Anger thrummed in the duke's voice and Stephen tempered his answer.

He slumped back in his chair and sighed. "Her father owes me funds. She's my leverage in getting it." He didn't point out that the day he'd gone to Arabella's father to ask for the blunt in a gentlemanlike manner, he'd spotted her in the garden and his whole plan to be civil had dissolved before his eyes. She'd been sitting on a bench, surrounded by lush green plants and he'd wanted her instantly. Had abruptly turned about and devised a more devious plan that would enable him to have her in his bed and alone for some weeks.

He was a cad.

And revenge was sweet. What he hadn't planned on was how the lovable woman with a strong backbone and warmth could worm her way under his ribs. He rubbed his chest, his like for her much more than he'd ever thought possible.

"She's a gentleman's daughter. You'll ruin her, if you haven't already. You are better than this, Stephen. I know you have peerage in your family. You need to act the gentleman, now man, before it's too late." The duke rubbed his jaw, his face all hard angles and serious.

The disappointment in his friend's tone ripped him in two. Was he better than this? His family had lost everything before he was even born. He'd never been given the opportunity to know what it was like to be lord and master of all he surveyed. To care for people as only a member of the upper ten-thousand should. So was he really better than a smuggling pirate who idled his life away on the sea? "You've always held me in too higher regard, Gabe. And let's not forget the woman you married was an innocent on her way back to England when you seduced her, in front of us all. How is what I'm doing any different?"

"I married Eloise, that's how it's different." The duke's face softened, but for only a moment. "It also doesn't hurt that I'm the Duke of Dale. You must take Miss Hester back to London and find another way to gain payment from her father."

Stephen cringed at the thought. He didn't want to return her. And what the hell did that mean if he did not?

Did he feel more for Arabella than he was admitting to himself? They certainly worked well together in bed, but in everyday life was another matter entirely. All Stephen knew was he was not ready for her to leave him. Not yet at least. "I will not. She stays with me until payment is made in full. I have nothing left to lose. But I'll be damned if I'll let my men suffer the same fate."

"You can still lose your life. Think man, not even I could save you from the noose should you be caught. And I haven't told you everything I've heard. There is more you need to know."

Stephen sat forward, frowning. "What don't I know?"

"Lord Montague has sailed after you and is headed here. Been tipped off somehow as to your location I would think. From what I could find out, he's crossed paths with Sir Hester who is now accompanying him. By tomorrow afternoon your captive's betrothed will be here to collect his bride-to-be." He paused, shaking his head. "This is absurd behavior. You know better than this." The duke gestured with his hands and looked ready to throttle him at his continued silence. "What possessed you?"

Stephen crossed his arms over his chest. "I will not be threatened by a fellow who likes to be buggered every night in the hells of London. A lifetime with me would be sweeter than a day with him. Why, he'd never even see her. Not the real, Arabella. He would only ever view her as a woman who took his freedom away. A woman who'll never be a man; the sex he desires most." He could not give Arabella over to such a fate. To sail away knowing he would never see her again and that he'd left her to life a life she would never enjoy.

A muscle worked at the duke's temple. "Whether the rumors are true or not, she's promised to him. Should he come here, you'd be best to hand her over and make your way to Scotland where the law will not find you too quickly or better yet, will forget your indiscretion. You know what Lord Montague is like. He's a prick with a lot of connections. Forget the blunt you're owed. Your life is worth more than a couple thousand pounds."

Stephen swallowed. Gabe was right in many respects. He should never have kidnapped Arabella in the first place. He pinched his nose. What the hell had gotten into him? But it still didn't change the fact he couldn't regret the decision he made. He would never regret his time with Arabella. They were the best times of his pitiful life so far. "I won't let her go."

"Even if Lord Montague is willing to settle the debt? What will your excuse be then to keep her?"

"It won't come to that. I shouldn't think Lord Montague wants to marry her that badly, especially as she's not his preferred type." Stephen took a long swig of his brandy. "If the debt is paid, of course I'll have to let her go. What reason would I have to keep her here then?" *Other than love…*

The duke nodded, his gaze compassionate. "Indeed."

"Tomorrow we should know." Stephen pushed away the thought that tonight could possibly be the last time he was ever with Arabella. Such musings didn't warrant thinking over.

"That you're having dinner with the chit, conversing with her and no doubt warming her bed at night tells me your indifference to what tomorrow could bring is false." He sighed. "That is all I'll say on the matter, but you need to take care. This could end badly for her and yourself." The duke leaned back in his chair. "As you know, Eloise is with child and I must leave you tomorrow morn, but should you need me, you know where I am."

Stephen nodded. "Aye. I know and I thank you." He

poured them both another brandy and settled back in his chair changing the subject to discuss their mutual interests in investments in London. He tried to concentrate on what his friend was saying, but his mind kept venturing upstairs to where Arabella slept waiting for him…

…possibly for the very last time.

He inwardly swore and left the duke, mouth agape, alone to converse with himself.

S he was asleep when he made it up to their room. The moonlight cast a hazy shade of blue over the covers highlighting her silky, white skin. Her hair looked ebony and cascaded over the pillows to frame her beautiful face. The bedding had slipped low on her chest, giving him an ample view of her nakedness and his cock twitched.

He sighed knowing he'd made a mess of things. He should never have kidnapped her and dragged her back to England with the sole purpose of ruining her and her family. Because now, that's exactly what would happen should the scandal break out across London.

If it hadn't already.

She fidgeted in sleep and her eyes fluttered open. She sat up and kneeled on the bed, beckoning him to join her. Stephen needed no cajoling and went to her willingly, took her mouth in a searing kiss and dragged them both into an inferno of desire.

After the weeks of being together, she'd learned a few things and quickly she disposed of his jacket, pulling his shirt out of his trews before sliding her hand inside and clasping his ass.

Stephen grinned through her fun. His body ached to take her, to lift her up and impale her on his hardened shaft. Playfully she pushed him away a little and slowly lifted her shift, exposing a body that had captivated him from the first moment he'd seen it.

Unable to stop himself he toppled her onto the bed and wrapped her legs about his waist. His cock slid against her moistened heat, teasing them both for what was to come.

Them. Literally.

She sighed his name and his control snapped. He thrust within her over and over again, the frenzied need thrumming through him unable to sate. She met his every stroke with awe, her gasps, moans for more and scoring nails down his back only making the interlude hotter, more enjoyable.

Her fingers tangled in his hair, tugging slightly. Stephen kissed his way down her neck, slender shoulder to eventually pay homage to her breasts. A lovely handful with nipples the color of roses on a summer's day.

She squirmed as his kisses moved farther down her person. Her stomach was smooth, soft and a beacon for more delights. Stephen pushed her legs apart, inhaling her sweet scent before kissing the glistening flesh before him.

"What are you doing? You can't do that."

He chuckled at the shocked but inquisitive tenor of her voice. "Lay back. Relax and let me love you."

Gradually the muscles in her legs relaxed. To have her, laying before him, open and trusting was the most delicious elixir he'd ever tasted. He licked her swollen bud and she gasped, her fingers clasping his head for purchase.

He loved her with his tongue, welcomed the rhythm she found undulating against his face. He added his hand to her lovemaking and took her with his fingers. Arabella lost all inhibitions and Stephen's body ached with the need to have her. How he adored her reaction to him, her enjoyment as great as his own. He groaned as her body tightened and then convulsed under his touch.

"That's it," he said, sucking on her hardened nub. "Come for me. Enjoy me as much as I am enjoying you." She whimpered under him, their lovemaking climaxing to a frenzy unlike any he'd ever experienced before. Arabella called his name and she came apart in his arms.

Stephen's body roared with the need to have her now. He sat up and flipped her over onto her stomach, before coming down over her back licking his way up her spine as he thrust deep into her hot wet core. The delighted gasp sent shivers to wrack his body. Sweat poured over his skin.

His release flowed through every limb, every pore before lights burst before his eyes as he came inside her. They laid like that for a while both lost in the exquisite torture that they had just endured. He slumped down next to her and pulled her against his chest, wanting her as close as he possibly could get to the woman in his arms.

She wrapped her arms around his body. "That was amazing Stephen. I can't imagine ever finding that with anybody else. Please tell me you do not experience this each time you lay with other women?"

Stephen shut his eyes. Did he experience this with other women when he slept with them? Something told him deep down inside is soul he didn't. That he'd never experienced anything so mind numbingly good in his eight and twenty years. "No. Never like this."

He felt rather than saw her smile against his chest. "Good."

CHAPTER 7

Arabella woke to the delicious sight of Stephen's bottom going into his breeches as he pulled them on. She lay there silently, loving the peaceful quietness of the morning and just the two of them being alone like a married couple partaking in a holiday by the seaside.

She shouldn't delude herself. All of it, their time together, the enjoyment they brought to one another, wasn't real. It wouldn't last. How could it when she was to marry another and Stephen had plans of his own future?

He busied himself about the room, pulling on his shirt, his boots, tying a cravat. There was no doubt she didn't know everything about him, but given time she was sure she would find out. Not that any time was left. Tears threatened and she blinked quickly, not wanting him to see her upset.

Not entirely certain of what he would do with her, she pushed the worrisome thoughts aside and continued to take pleasure in the view. Stephen bent over and his pants pulled tight. A smiled lifted her lips. He really was the most handsome rogue she'd ever seen.

And he was hers to enjoy, if only for the day.

He turned and caught her staring. A knowing eyebrow rose as he strode toward the bed. "Like what you see, Miss Hester?"

She kneeled and let the sheet fall to the bed. He stilled, his muscles tightening as if preparing to launch and tackle her to the ground. The thought of what he did to her, the pleasure each touch wrought made the imagining longed for. "As a matter of fact I do." She pulled him closer by the waist of his pants. "In fact, perhaps you would be inclined to forgo whatever business takes you from me and join me here for some other mutual satisfaction."

He chuckled, his touch idly gliding up and down her back. She shivered and let her own hand venture over his frontfalls. He cock hardened against her palm and her body warmed in response.

"I want you, Stephen." A muscle twitched in his jaw before, without any notice, he flipped her onto her back, came down on top of her and ground himself against her. Arabella gasped at the contact, wanting, needing him close. The non-existent distance too much to bear.

He ripped at his frontfalls, lifted her a little and thrust into her aching core and carried them both toward bliss within moments. She came up to meet him, to join with him as deep as possible. He filled her completely, made her whole and she moaned when he slowed his pace to tease relentlessly.

"Don't stop," she gasped. He didn't, just inexorably kept up his torturous pace.

"I won't," he whispered against her ear. "Not until you ask me to." He nipped her lobe, his hands either side of her skull. She met his gaze and almost drowned in his sensual haze. They watched each other as both fell into bliss. The delicious spasms that rocked through her body left her sated and sleepy. Arabella kissed his shoulder, loving the feel of Stephen above her, in her, with her.

"I never knew it could be like this for a woman. That being with a man could be so enjoyable."

Stephen's lips curved and then he laughed. "If the man's doing it right of course it can. I'm glad I'm able to pleasure you." He laid beside her, pulling her into the crook of his arm. "You're a very intelligent, beautiful woman who deserves only the best of all things."

Arabella looked up and held his gaze. "I'm glad you think so. Thank you."

He nodded. "I do. Don't ever think otherwise."

She snuggled into his hold, not wanting him to see that she'd become a watering pot since last night. The realization that she did not want to leave Stephen hit her like gale force wind on the stormy seas. He was everything she wanted in life. A man who listened to her, loved her with reverence and only wanted what was best. And soon she would have to leave him. Family duty told her so, along with marriage contracts, but the thought of never seeing him again tore her in two.

Broke her heart in fact.

CHAPTER 8

Stephen crossed his arms over his chest and glared at the pompous Lord Montague, who stood on the deck of his own ship, similarly glaring. "So what do we owe the pleasure, my lord? I didn't think the coastal communities of Cornwall would pull such a gentleman of the *ton* to its ports. You'll find no Almacks here."

His lordship snarled and Stephen laughed. He almost didn't recognize Lord Montague. In the months since he'd seen him, he'd grown larger, more pompous and red-faced. "Where is Miss Hester? I'm here to take her home. We're to be married next week." His voice was high, too high for a man.

"Take a breath lad. You are allowed to breathe you know." Stephen leaned against the railing and heard the footsteps of two of his crewmen come to stand behind him. Lord Montague for all his feminine characteristics had two very beefy crew members watching the proceedings from behind his lordship. It didn't tax Stephen's imagination to know the men were trouble. It was best to have his own protection in situations like these.

An older man he recognized as Arabella's father appeared on deck and waddled over to where her betrothed stood. "Where is my daughter? I demand you release her at once."

Lord Montague lifted his overly long nose in the air. "Do not assume I'm here to spar with you. I'm here for my betrothed and nothing more. Now, where is she?"

"Safe." Stephen raised his brow. "Next question."

"It's not a question but a command. Bring her to me post haste and no further action will be taken against you. Not by me at least."

Arabella's father huffed out a breath. "I, on the other hand, will ensure you pay for this treachery."

"I look forward to it, Sir Hester," Stephen said. "But pray tell me, Lord Montague, why is it that a man of your ilk wishes to marry at all? I always thought your tastes veered in another direction entirely."

His lordships face turned crimson. "You have one hour to produce Miss Hester or I'll not be held responsible for what happens to you, your men or your ship."

Stephen waved the man's threats away. "An hour? But I have to say my goodbyes and we're forgetting one very important factor in all this. The payment that is due to me." Lord Montague nodded to one of his men who quickly ran off. The fact that the payment of two thousand pounds was only moments away should accelerate the blood pumping through Stephens veins. He should be happy, elated that his men would have the future they'd worked so hard to grasp.

It didn't. If anything the thought of the payment was like the bemoaning sound of a church death knell. It meant the end of his time with Arabella. Panic mixed with pain coursed through his gut. He may never see her again. Kiss lips that bespoke of sin and felt like silk. Listen to the intelligent quick wit that had captured his attention from the very first.

He would miss her, and something deep within his mind whispered that he'd do a lot more than that. He'd be only half of himself without her.

I love her.

The realization struck him like a sword to the throat. He loved her? The words that should frighten him didn't. Instead they fit him like a new pair of leather boots.

The brute who ran off returned.

"Give Captain Blackmore the bag," Lord Montague said without emotion.

Arabella's father gestured at the bag as it was handed over. "I had the funds in Malta, should you have just asked, none of this would've been necessary against my daughter. But like the thieving, kidnapping scoundrel that you are, you couldn't wait like any other patient man. No. Instead you kidnapped an innocent woman and tried to ruin her reputation."

Stephen's eyes narrowed as his temper started to spike. "I don't take well to liars, and you Sir Hester, are one of those. I have waited a good twelve months for this payment, none of which was forthcoming until today and not until I had to take action totally against my better judgment or character." He fought the ill ease that sat in his gut. Yes, he'd waited months for payment, but the action to kidnap Arabella couldn't be laid at anyone's door but his own. And sinner that he was, he'd enjoyed every damn moment with the lass.

Stephen's second in command took the bag and rifled through it. "Looks to be all here, Captain."

Stephen nodded. "Put it below decks."

Lord Montague stepped forward. "Your time is running out Captain Blackmore. I want to see my betrothed. Now." Stephen raised his brow at the man's attempt to sound threatening. What a sad little specimen his lordship was.

"Go fetch Arabella and gather up anything she has at the inn and on the ship. She's leaving forthwith," Stephen barked out the order to a member of his crew and hated the way his voice strained over the word 'leaving'.

His lordship smirked. "I'm so glad you've seen reason. Common sense is not something I would associate with a pirate, but in your case and in this instance you seem to have some."

"I would shut up and rightly so, Lord Montague, before I'm tempted to step onto your ship and cut off the one appendage you love most. And as for you, Sir Hester. I'm not without connections also, with a few whispered words I could ruin you in London. Best you shut up as well."

Both men paled and didn't reply.

It took an hour or so for Arabella to be rowed out to the anchored ships. During the time the men on both ships stood about, patiently waiting, but always on alert. Stephen watched as she climbed up the rope latter and came to stand beside him on his deck. She had a small bag clasped in her hand and a becoming flush on her cheeks. Her hair curled about her shoulders, accentuating the lovely curve of her neck. His body tightened at the sight of her. Possibly his last.

His mind fought a war within itself. Could he ask her to leave all that she aspired to, had promised herself, to marry him instead? To live in Scotland, an isolated wilderness far from the polished delights of London for the rest of her days?

And what about the funds? Was it more important to him and his men than Arabella?

He inwardly swore at the crossroad he now found himself and having no idea on which direction to take.

※

The sound of excited voices from the street below woke Arabella with a start. She scrambled out of bed and ran to the window to see what was happening. From the room's view, she could see Stephen's ship anchored off the bay, with another ship close beside it.

Trepidation clawed at her innards over who was docked beside him although she could probably guess. The distance not so very far, she could make out Stephen on his deck surrounded by his crewmen. The gentleman on the other ship remained unknown.

Arabella dressed and went to leave, only to find her room door locked. Concern for Stephen warred with annoyance at his high-handedness at locking her in again.

Going back to the window she watched as the two men traded words to one another. She narrowed her eyes trying to focus better, and swore when the other gentleman turned and she recognized Lord Montague.

Blast and the devil he was here and if the tubby gentleman coming to stand beside him was any indication, so was her father!

The thought of his lordship organizing a rescue almost made her laugh. Lord Montague was a man who loathed anything remotely distasteful. No doubt a rescue where his coattails could become sullied was classed as such.

Their appearance could only mean one thing. She was leaving. And did she even wish to any longer? Being with Stephen had been an exciting journey she'd never thought possible. It may not have started out too well, but the nights of pleasure and days of adventure had soon brought them together and for her at least, made her see him in a different perspective.

He was everything to her. Meant the world to her.

I love him...

One of Stephen's men broke away and started down the rope ladder, getting into the small wooden craft tied to the ship before rowing toward shore. Arabella fumbled about for her meagre belongings just in case Stephen wished her to come aboard.

She stopped what she was doing and realized where her thoughts had taken her. She loved him, that she was certain, but to leave with him? Embark on a life that was as uncertain as the weather was another thing entirely.

Could she do it? Really? Could she choose love and adventure, losing all that she'd been brought up to be, a respectable, steady lady with morals for Stephen?

A knock sounded at her door just as she slipped on a pair of boots.

"The captain wishes you to join him on the ship, Miss Hester," a firm male voice said from behind the wood.

He unlocked the door and Arabella followed the deckhand. The trip out to the ship was reasonably quick and the closer they came, the easier it was to hear the two men and their war of words. Curses that were new to her, even after all the months on board a pirate's ship, volleyed from one boat to another. She shook her head at the absurdness.

Really. Men could be so immature at times.

"Gentleman, stop. Enough of this madness." Arabella climbed up the rope ladder and turned to Lord Montague as she made the deck. She smiled in welcome to her father. "What are you doing here? It never occurred to me that you would chase us down."

"You speak, daughter, as if you've enjoyed the company of the blasted rogue." Her father threw a disgusted look at Stephen. "Come aboard and quickly. The sooner we have you away from this man the better."

She didn't move as an abundance of thoughts, feelings and questions bombarded her mind. Not the least of them being how unwelcome Lord Montague's presence was now that he'd actually appeared. He was a sickly color, as if the rocking motion of the boat didn't mesh well with his stomach.

"Miss Hester, we're to return to London forthwith where with any luck, notice of your prolonged stay with Captain Blackmore will be washed away like the tide. We're to marry next week."

Stephen scoffed. "I can't help but think Arabella's fall from grace would suit you well. Admit it man, you don't want to marry her. And you know damn well as to why."

Arabella started at his words. She frowned. "Why wouldn't his lordship wish to marry me? I'm not abhorrent."

He looked from her to Lord Montague, his face more thunderous than the day she'd thrown the mop overboard. "Please enlighten us, my lord."

Her betrothed pulled at his neckcloth, sweat forming on his brow. "Don't be absurd. I love Miss Hester." His lordship gestured for her to come aboard. "Join me, my dear. We'll leave directly. Now that Captain Blackmore has been paid in full there is no more reason for you to stay."

Arabella raised her brow. Stephen already had the funds? So his use of her was at an end unless…

Stephen closed the short distance between them and clasped her hands. "You don't have to go. Stay with me. Be with me." His voice was low, desperate almost.

Hope bloomed in her chest. The image of a future with him was tempting. She doubted there would be a moment of boredom. He excited her, discussed things with her as an equal. Didn't treat her as some silly nitwit girl so many men seemed to do. And he was her lover…

Her father jumped from one ship to the other and strode toward her. Arabella shut her mouth with a snap not knowing her father could be so agile when so large. "Daughter, a word in private if you will." He took her arm and pulled her a good distance away from Stephen. "What is this madness? You cannot possibly be thinking of staying with this pirate." He spat the word out like salty seawater. "Your life is with me and your future husband. I command you to leave with us at once."

She stepped back and crossed her arms. "Why must I? What I feel for the captain far outweighs what I've ever felt for Lord Montague. And you're wealthy, there is no reason for me to marry his lordship. We could make up some sort of excuse as to my disappearance from society. Say I stayed in Malta due to some sickly ailment or some such."

"Don't be absurd child. You cannot just disappear!" Her father waved his hands about in agitation. "I think it's time to tell you as to why you must leave." He sighed. "My pockets are to let. Other than the house in London, which I transferred into your name two years ago, nothing we own will remain ours unless you marry Lord Montague." Her father pulled out his handkerchief and wiped his brow, his face a deep ruddy color. "I've gambled us into a vicious debt that I cannot pay. Your betrothed has promised all vowels will be paid in full should you marry him. I owe a lot of men a lot of blunt."

So it was true. Her father was a liar and a gambler and they were poor. Despair washed over her knowing she couldn't let her father become ruined. "Why would Lord Montague do this for us? I certainly don't believe it's because he's in love with me." Her father licked his lips in agitation. "Answer me, Father?"

He sighed. "The reasons behind Lord Montague wishing to marry you are his and only his. He has not shared them with me. When the contracts were signed, let me assure you, both of us were pleased with the outcome. You will have a good life with him."

"I still don't see why I should go. So we're not as wealthy as we used to be, but there are worse prospects for people I'm sure. You can live with me and Captain Blackmore," she pleaded, wanting to hold onto her dream of marrying Stephen, if he'd have her.

Tears welled in her father's eyes and Arabella's heart twisted. "Would you see me in a poor house? After all the years I raised you, loved you only as a father can and you would turn your back on me when I needed you most. Please, Arabella, don't do this to me. Please marry his lordship. I beg of you."

Pounding started to thump across her brow. She rubbed her temples to try and alleviate the pain. She couldn't betray her father. Yes, he'd made mistakes, but he'd been the best parent anyone could ask for. She could not allow his future to be uncertain and unpleasant. She nodded, family duty outweighing that of her heart's desire. "I will do as you ask. Go back to the ship and I'll join you shortly."

He nodded, wiping his eyes before waddling off.

Stephen joined her and the worry she could read in his eyes tore at her heart. Tore at her own for that matter. "Our time has been wonderful and I thank you for it, but you know I cannot stay. I must go." Arabella tried to keep her voice strong, determined, but even she could hear the wavering tempo of devastation in it.

He stared at her in shocked silence for a moment. "Why can you not? I may not be able to give you a position, title or extreme wealth, but you have my heart. Is that not enough?"

Arabella bit her lip. Had he just told her he loved her? Tears welled in her eyes and her knees threatened to give way. He loved her. "I've already broken too many vows. One major one being with you, enjoying you in the way only a wife should enjoy a husband. I cannot break my understanding with Lord Montague as well. The banns have been called. All of London is expecting me to become his wife. My father—"

"Is no longer with funds as I said once before, but now has decided to use this against you to make you marry a man you do not love." Stephen shook her a little. "You cannot do this, Arabella. Not to yourself. You deserve better than this." Desperation tinged his tone and his eyes beseeched her to see sense.

"He's my father." Tears spilled over knowing she was leaving the man she loved. A man who loved her. She sniffed. "I cannot break my promise."

Stephen rubbed his jaw, shaking his head. "Stop and think for a moment. Why would a wealthy man marry a poor woman when he does not have to? He does not love you, so why the need to marry? Perhaps on your journey back to the capitol you should ask your father to explain this phenomenon." Sarcasm laced his tone and Arabella frowned. What was he getting at?

"What are you trying to say? That my father is in some way blackmailing Lord Montague? His lordship is above reproach. There is nothing my father could use against him." Arabella started toward the other ship. How could Stephen think so lowly of her only family? It was beyond insulting. But then, he was a pirate after all. A man used to using any underhanded tactic in getting his own way.

"So a life of luxury and leisure is more important than

honor? Am I correct in assuming that? I cannot say I'm not disappointed in you, my dear. I didn't think you were materialistic. I suppose I'm not such a good judge of character." Stephen did not follow her, and yet his words hit her like a whip.

Turning to face him she started at the anger she read in his gaze. "I hardly think you're a beacon on which others should strive for regarding good character and judgment." Disdain laced her tone. "You kidnapped me. Seduced me if you wish to throw stones at my head." Arabella hated that she was saying such things that were not the truth. The day she gave herself to Stephen, she did so willingly. "I never asked for this. I never asked to be taken away from the only life I knew. To be thrust on to the high seas with a pirate and his raggedy crew. And here you stand, upset and angry at me when I must refuse your charms, no matter how tempting, because I made a promise to someone else, long before I met you. You are being unfair," her voice broke and she fought to breathe.

"I'm being unfair?" He yelled, the men on the ship making themselves scarce. "I love you and you're choosing to walk away from that for the sake of your father's comfort, because let me assure you, *Miss Hester*, there will never be any love in your marriage. You will be used as a cover for Lord Montague's real desires and little else. I mourn the life you will lead. It will not be the one you've always wished for."

Arabella threw her belongings onto Lord Montague's ship. Her hands shook and she fisted them at her sides to stop the trembling. How she wanted to run to him, to say yes to all that he offered and let her father, her betrothed sort out their own mess. "Goodbye and good luck Captain Blackmore. I wish you well."

He bestowed a sweeping bow. "I don't need any luck,

Miss Hester. You keep it. I feel you'll need it a lot more than I."

Arabella's father laughed. "You can try and run but the authorities will catch up with you to seek my revenge. Perhaps I may visit you in Newgate."

"There will be no authorities or further discussion involving them in relation to the captain." She turned and met her father's startled eye. "Push the subject and I will not marry Lord Montague under any circumstance. Do you understand, Father?"

He nodded, helped her board the other ship and pulled her toward the stairs to go below deck. At the threshold, Arabella turned to see a quick exchange between Lord Montague and Stephen. Her stomach rolled with nerves at having to leave the man she loved. Of course she'd always known the time would come when she would go, but it didn't make that time any easier when it arrived.

Her father of course wished for his daughter's happiness, no matter the circumstances or cost to the family. He'd brought her up to think this way, but it would seem when the time came for such choices, men were want to change their minds.

Stephen did not look her way again, and she bit back the tears that threatened. This would be the last time she'd ever see him. In her mind's eye, she captured an image of him, every curve, every nuance of his being before he shouted out commands to set sail before disappearing below decks. Out of sight and out of her life. Forever.

CHAPTER 9

Arabella looked down at her simple blue morning gown and wiped away tears that refused to stop. The past four weeks without Stephen, without waking up next to him, talking to him, laughing with him had been the worst of her life.

She'd made a mistake and now it was too late to change her mind.

"The carriage is here, Arabella. We must leave," her father said, cold and autocratic as it had been from the moment they stepped foot in London. Not that she cared any longer. One could not care when one no longer had a heart that beat.

She stood and followed her father downstairs and toward the front door. Their two newly hired footmen bowed as she went past and she cringed at the extravagant lifestyle her father had started to live since her betrothal to Lord Montague was secured.

Stephen had been right all along. Her father had a problem handling money, and if his expenditures over the past few weeks were any indication it wouldn't take him very long to go through what blunt Lord Montague had as well.

She could almost feel sorry for her future husband… should he ever bother to visit her, that was. Not once since she'd been thrust into a carriage on the docks had he come to see her. Yes, missives were sent, notifying her of what he expected her to wear on their wedding day. The rules she should follow once his bride. The most glaringly obvious one being she was not to ask for consummation of the marriage until he was ready. Not that she wanted to sleep with the prig in any case. Even the thought of kissing the man after their wedding sent revulsion to her core.

And yet she wondered at his lordships decree that he would not sleep with her. What gentleman wasn't ready to claim his wife? None of it made any sense and Stephen's cryptic words flittered through her mind. What was it that she wasn't seeing.

She climbed into the carriage and settled back into the leather squabs as her father fussed with his cravat. "Not long now, my dear. I'm so pleased I'll be able to call you Lady Montague. It has a certain ring about it, don't you think?"

A terrible one perhaps… "Yes, Father, it's most exciting." Her voice dripped with boredom, something she had an inkling her life was going to be from now on. So different to what her life with Stephen might have been. Where was he right at this moment? Was he happy, sad, a thousand miles away on a distant ocean…?

The ride to St James was quick and before long Arabella made her way toward the large double wooden doors. Music started to play as she entered, her hand nestled softly over her father's. It would be a perfect day, a perfect wedding should she be marrying the man she loved.

But she was not. What a fool she'd been to think putting someone else's wants and desires above her own heart. Lord Montague didn't care for her and never would and she was being sold to the highest bidder, and all to keep her father accustomed to a lifestyle he could no longer afford.

Lord Montague looked stunning in his cream satin knee-breeches, perfectly cut blue coat and buckled shoes. He didn't bother to turn and watch her walk toward him. Instead his back was severely straight, rigid to the point of looking painful.

Her father gave her over to his lordship and returned to the pew. Arabella nodded to the priest for him to begin. She wouldn't look at Lord Montague. How could she? They were not a good match and nor did she desire him to be her husband. A role she loathed to think on and did not want. If she were truthful with herself, probably never wanted. Back in Malta when he had asked for her hand, she'd been so overjoyed a lord had asked to marry her, she had forgotten to ask herself if she cared that he did. Her father was certainly pleased, which made her also, but thinking back Arabella realized she didn't care at all for his lordship. Nor ever would.

They started to take their vows, repeating what the priest said to them. Compelled to look at his lordship, she was surprised to see the ashen and fear in Lord Montague's eyes as if he too was having second thoughts. Hope bloomed in her heart. Maybe there was a chance for all to see sense before it was too late.

She squeezed his hand. "Are you well, my lord?"

His attention wavered from her to her father's, the fear in his eyes increasing. "Of course, my dear. Just nervous, I believe."

The priest coughed and she glared at the man of the cloth who rolled his eyes.

Arabella shook her head. "No, it's not just nerves. You do not want to marry me any more than I wish to marry you." She turned to her father, done with all the secrets, and pretending all of this was acceptable. "What is going on here that I don't know about?"

"What do you mean? Proceed this instant. You're embarrassing the family."

She scoffed. "How can I embarrass anyone? There isn't anybody here to see." She turned back to his lordship. "Do you want to marry me, Frederick? And I want the truth."

His shoulders slumped, and he shook his head. "I do not." He took her hand. "There is something your father knows about me that he's blackmailing me with," he said, whispering the words so her father would not hear. "My lifestyle has never involved plans of marriage, but when one isn't careful enough, one can find oneself before a priest marrying a woman, no matter how lovely, that is not who he loves."

Realization struck her like a blow. How could she not have seen it? She nodded, understanding dawning on her over what Stephen was trying to warn her of all those weeks ago. "I will not marry you, my lord. Not today or ever." She smiled, hugging his lordship for the first time since their betrothal. "Whatever my father has threatened you with you must forget. I will not allow you to be a part of his deviant money-making schemes."

"What the hell do you think you're doing, child!" Her father scrambled toward them and clasped her arm. She bit back a whimper as his hold increased with every word. "I will ruin him should you not do as you're told. We'll be finished should you refuse to marry this man. Do you know what that means?"

Arabella wrenched her arm free, seeing her father clearly for the first time. A swindler, a pirate far worse than Stephen ever could be. "Of course I do, but I also know it's time you held yourself accountable for the way you live your life. Lord Montague should not be your bank just because you assume to know something of his life."

Her father's face mottled in anger, his skin turning as red as a lobster. "I forbid you to leave this church unmarried. I'm your father, the head of our household. You will do as you're told." His words thundered through the church and out the corner of her eye Arabella noted the priest jumped.

"I will not." Arabella stood nose to nose with him and refused to give in to her churning stomach. She'd never stood up for herself in such a way in her life. And although liberating, it was also terrifying. She supposed all her weeks with Stephen had given her the strength of mind to call out a wrong when she saw one. Not to sit idly by and allow bad things to happen, but to change them, make situations better if possible. "You cannot make me do something I disagree with. Not to mention threatening Lord Montague as well. How could you act so low? You're behaving in a way I'm unfamiliar with. Where is the loving, caring father that I know?"

"Finished, that's where," he shouted before his eyes widened in shock.

Arabella clasped her father's arm as he swayed. His knees buckled under his weight and she screamed for Lord Montague's help as her father crumbled to the cold, tiled floor.

Commotion erupted behind her, the priest yelling for the altar boys to run for help. Arabella patted his cheek, trying to rouse him in any way she could. "Father? Wake up. Are you all right? Please talk to me."

He moaned but reached out to take her hand. "My chest. Pain," he mumbled, closing his eyes again.

Lord Montague placed his coat beneath her father's head. Arabella didn't know what to do or how to help him. She called out for water, but her parent just pushed it away when she went to help him drink.

"Please, Father. What can I do? What's happening?" She sniffed, the thought that he was dying before her eyes more than she could bear. He couldn't leave her after such a fight. For all his trouble making, his wayward lifestyle, he was her papa. She loved him. "What can we do?"

He shook his head, clasping his chest. "I'm sorry Arabella."

She kissed his cheek and hugged him. "I'm sorry too. I love you. Please don't leave me." Arabella sobbed as the last beat of her father's heart thumped beneath her ear, before silence reigned. She lay there, the thought that she'd lost the last member of her family and in such a way, under such terrible circumstances beyond comprehension.

Lord Montague pulled her away and gave comfort as best he could. "It'll be all right, Arabella. I'll ensure you will be fully taken care of."

She sobbed against his chest. Even after all her father had put this man through he'd still ensure her well-being. Perhaps her opinion of his lordship was wrong. "No. You don't have to. This is not your responsibility. You've been too kind after everything I've put you through. How will I ever thank you?"

He pulled out a handkerchief and wiped her tears. "No thanks are needed." A group of men, one carrying a bag and Arabella assumed to be a doctor, ran into the church. She sat on a pew knowing there wasn't anything they could do for her father.

Guilt over their fight, one of the last moments she had

with the man who raised her tore at her soul. How could she be so heartless?

"I will not let you think this is your fault." Lord Montague sat beside her. "The doctor is saying it looks like he's had a heart seizure of some kind. I can see by your face you're blaming yourself and you should not. Terrible tragedies happen, my dear. No one is to blame."

"But I fought with him, made his temper rise more than I should."

"And rightly so. What your father was doing was wrong and you're a remarkable woman having stood up for me and your life like you did." His lordship took her hand, patting it kindly. "Do not forget he apologized, Arabella. He knew within himself that what he was doing was wrong. Please do not blame yourself about what has transpired here today. It could've happened anywhere and at any time."

The doctor echoed Lord Montague's words, but it still didn't make the passing of her only living parent easier. From this moment on, she was truly alone. Even Stephen was lost to her and his lordship would no doubt go on with his life less a wife just as he should.

What would she do? Where would she go? Once her father's debts were settled by the sale of their London home, she'd be homeless, friendless even. To cry off a marriage to a peer of the realm was no small thing. From this day forward, she would truly be ruined.

Tears streamed down her cheeks. Sure, she had wished for freedom to choose her own future, to pick her own husband and the sort of life she wanted to lead, but never at the cost of her father's life.

Never that.

CHAPTER 10

Stephen strolled across a paddock covered with heather and wildflowers which would, over the next few weeks, give way to a highland winter. And if the chilling wind from the north was any indication, this year may the coldest he'd had to live through in many years.

Sailing and living mostly in foreign places with sandy beaches and a warm sun on his back was a pleasant distant memory that haunted him. Well, it would haunt him until his body acclimatized to Scotland. He'd never known such a cold place and yet he would not wish to be anywhere else in the world.

In the distance rose the small castle he now called home. The brown and gold stone a beacon in the otherwise green landscape. It was all he had now. Having sold his ship to give his men the future they deserved, the funds that were left over were soon eaten up with the repairs he'd had to make to the leaking castle roof.

The home farms should start to make profit again and even though there wasn't a lot of blunt left from his smuggling days, it was enough to keep him and his mother, who'd he'd moved up here as well, reasonably comfortable for a year or two until the estate was self-sufficient once more.

A distant rumble sounded in the south and he turned to peer at the only road that ran into his property. He frowned having not expected anyone of than the Duke of Dale, who wasn't due to arrive for some weeks.

A carriage, covered with dust and mud from the unforgiving Scottish highland roads materialized after coming around the last curve in the road. The cattle looked well defined and expensive. Maybe Gabe had come early.

He made his way toward the house by following an old sheep track that wound its way down the hillside. The staff came out to greet the vehicle and to help the occupants to step down.

Stephen's step faltered when a vision in an emerald green traveling gown alighted and looked about with interest. Instead of her long brown locks falling loose about her shoulders, they were coiled up into a coiffure on top of her head.

He continued walking on, watching her, taking his fill of the one woman he'd longed to see more than the highlands sunrise.

Arabella…

She followed his footman into the house and he lost sight of her. Stephen went around the back of the house, dropped the game birds he'd been able to kill in to the kitchens, and notified cook that he'd have a guest at dinner.

The jovial woman took the news with aplomb and busied herself with renewed vigor having someone other than his mother and himself to cook for.

Stephen headed for the front drawing room, once the castle's old solar and entered without knocking. Arabella stood beside the bookcase that covered one whole wall, her attention riveted on the works of the greats. "Good afternoon, Lady Montague. I had not expected to see you again." He shut the door, seating himself at the desk while trying to busy himself with the mail with little success. The thought she was here, married and no longer accessible to him drove him insane.

It was not to be borne. He closed his eyes for a moment, and fought for calm lest he throw his blotter against the wall or something even more ridiculous.

"Hello, Stephen." She sat in the chair before his desk and smiled. "I'm sorry to intrude on you without notice, but I was afraid you wouldn't see me if I wrote and notified you of my intention to call."

"And what possibly could be your intention? I believe everything we've said to one another has left no stone unturned." She paled a little at his words and he wanted to go to her, to hold her, comfort her in any way he could. Stephen gritted his teeth and didn't move.

"You never told me about your lineage or about this ancestral home you've purchased since your grandfather lost it all at a game of cards."

Stephen started. Not many knew that's why. "I see you've been talking to the Duke of Dale."

She gave a decisive nod. "I have. And what a tale of woe he told me." A small frown line appeared between her perfect brows. "Why did you never tell me?"

Just the thought of how low the family had fallen left him hollow inside. "No one knows, and I don't like talking about my family or their fall from grace. Life on the sea was the only option left for me and I made the most of it. I may no longer have a title, but I have my ancestral home back. I'm satisfied."

"For what it's worth, I'm proud of your accomplishments. You have not had the easiest life, and yet you still achieved your goals. I too can only wish that should my situation ever be similar that I would act the same. Not settle for less than what I deserve."

A lump formed in Stephen's throat having not expected to hear such pride in her words. Nor that Arabella's belief in him was so important. Yet, it was.

"Are you angry I came? I thought…" her voice trailed off and she fidgeted with the hem of her glove.

"What, Miss Hester?"

Arabella stood and went to the sideboard and after pouring herself a brandy, downed it in one swallow. She coughed before walking over to him, rolling back his chair and sitting before him on his desk.

Stephen's body thrummed in anticipation. There was never any doubt Arabella could be a seductive minx when she wished, but he never thought she'd be so once married. Had she married him at least he'd never allow her out of his sight. Lord Montague was a fool who didn't know a gem when he held one in his hand. "What are you doing?" He cleared his throat, his voice sounding even tight to his own ears.

"I want you. All of you." She sat on his lap and pushed a lock of hair out of his eyes. "I never married Lord Montague. You are the man I want to marry and to spend the rest of my days with. It is you I love." Stephen watched her a moment, read the sincerity in her gaze. *She never married Lord Montague?*

He pulled back, startled by her words. "What happened?" Sadness clouded her eyes and he frowned. "Tell me what happened, Arabella."

She sighed. "The wedding went ahead as planned. I would do my duty for my father, but as I was walking down the aisle, no guests present to celebrate our wedding and my betrothed who looked like I was a noose about his neck

I realized I couldn't do it. I couldn't put another person's happiness before my own. I was tired of being ordered about by the men in my life." She gave him a small smile. "I halted the ceremony and discussed my fears with Lord Montague. He was in agreement. It seems Father had been blackmailing him in relation to sexual trysts with men. I was horrified to find out Father had acted so low." She paused, her lip wobbling. "My father passed away."

Stephen swore, not believing what he was hearing. "Your father died! How?"

"He collapsed in the church, before Lord Montague and me. There was nothing we could do. A doctor said it was a heart seizure or possibly a problem within his brain." A tear slid down her cheek and Stephen wrenched her into his arms, trying to comfort her in any way he could.

How had he not heard of this? "Why did you not write? I would've come for you."

"I had to sell the London house as Father had placed it in my name to keep it from the debt collectors. There was so much to be done. The funeral, chasing down vowels and paying them in full. You were so right about what my father had been up to. I apologize for calling you a lying cad. You are not one." She nuzzled against his neck and he held her tighter, never wishing her to be parted from him again.

He smiled and kissed her, lingered as her sweetness burst through his soul like light. "I'm a cad, there is no doubt, but I'll never lie to you. I also want you to know these past weeks without you have been hellish. The thought of you belonging to another, and someone who would never treat you with reverence as I would drove me insane." He paused, catching her attention. "I never kept the payment from your father."

She started, her eyes wide with shock. "You didn't?"

"I did not," he said, shaking his head. "I sent it all back, every penny. You are worth more to me than any blunt that was owed, and the thought of taking payment in lieu of having you made me ill." He wiped a tear from her cheek. "I love you Arabella."

She hugged him about his neck and he could hear her smile in her words. "You love me? Is that all?"

"Greedy minx." He raised his brow. "What else would you like for me to say? Maybe…" he paused, grinning. "Will you marry me?" A light blush stole over her cheeks and Stephen had never seen anyone more beautiful.

"Yes. I will marry you, my gentleman pirate. And I will love you forever."

Stephen kissed her hard, reveled in the feel of her body against his chest, the only woman he ever wanted to feel again. He stood and lifted her onto the desk, quickly hiking up her traveling gown skirts. He had to have her. Here. Now. Later he would lay her down on his bed, pay homage to her delectable body, but right now, after weeks apart, his desire was too great.

She ripped at his frontfalls and Stephen gritted his teeth as her touch swept over his engorged cock. Damn it. He was so hard for her it hurt. He thrust into her waiting palm when she freed him and it was heaven on earth.

Cool air kissed his buttocks as his breeches fell to the floor. Stephen nibbled her chin as he slid her toward the edge of the desk. She laughed and wrapped her legs about his waist. "Damn, I want you. I don't know how gentle I'll be."

She clasped his back, her nails scoring his skin as she held him close. "I don't care. Do as you will."

Stephen positioned himself at her core, her heat, her readiness for him beyond his imaginings. What a marvelous woman and now she was his. Possession took hold and he slid easily and fully into her. Her body clasped him tight, drawing him toward a blissful end that he was determined she too would reach. Today was just the beginning of many tomorrows.

How lucky he was.

<hr />

Arabella moaned as Stephen finally claimed her. Their time a part felt like years. Had it really only been weeks? He thrust into her, his body a perfect fit. God she had missed him. Had missed the adventure he had wrapped around his soul.

And his love making was no different. Hot, hard and fulfilling seemed to be the man's motto. How lucky was she to have been kidnapped by him.

She played with his buttocks and forced him to take her just as she liked. Stephen's bed sport had always been exciting, but today it was different. There was an edge of possession mixed with desperation. A desperation born out of love and the thought that what one had and adored would never be theirs again. Arabella knew the emotion well, having lived the hell during their weeks apart. "Yes," she gasped as with each stroke he pushed her toward a pinnacle she longed to reach. He clasped her leg and changed the pace of their lovemaking, going slower but deeper each time.

Arabella threw her head back, her body coiling tight with impending release. There was something arousing being dressed but taken in full daylight and on a desk. Memories of such an escapade on Stephen's ship slipped through her mind and she smiled. What a fabulous life she was about to begin.

"Come for me, darling." He continued to take her, his

strong, capable hands biting in to her buttocks. "Let me feel you shatter around me."

His dirty talk inflamed her more. She held onto him, urged him to take her harder, faster. He did and within moments, the sensation of absolute bliss thrummed throughout her body. Arabella screamed his name, pulled him to her until he too exclaimed an echoing release.

They collapsed on his desk, both breathing hard as if they had run a thousand miles. Arabella smiled. "I'm going to enjoy being your wife. I think I will enjoy it very much." She met his gaze and read amusement in his blue eyes.

"That's just as it should be. I wouldn't have anything less for my bonny English lass," he said, teasing her with his Scottish brogue.

"And that's exactly why I'm yours. Forever."

He nodded, his face becoming serious. "Yes. Forever, and then some."

Dear Reader,

Thank you for taking the time to read *Her Gentleman Pirate*! I hope you enjoyed the second book in my High Seas & High Stakes series. If you haven't picked up book one, His Lady Smuggler, you can pick up your copy here.

I'm forever grateful to my readers, so if you're able, I would appreciate an honest review of *Her Gentleman Pirate*. As they say, feed an author, leave a review!

If you'd like to learn about book one in my Kiss the Wallflower series, *A Midsummer Kiss*, please read on. I have included chapter one for your reading pleasure.

Tamara Gill

A MIDSUMMER KISS

KISS THE WALLFLOWER, BOOK 1

Orphaned at a tender age, Miss Louise Grant spent her life in servitude to care for her younger siblings. Now, no longer needed as a duchess' companion, Louise has procured employment in York. But on her last night in London, her reputation is shattered when the drunk and disorderly Marquess mistakes Louise's room for his lover's.

. . .

Luke, the Marquess Graham is determined to never torment himself again by daring to love. Stumbling into Miss Louise Grant's room destroys his days of bachelorhood when he is pressured into marrying her. However, the cold and distant Marquess knows they'll never have a happy marriage; his new and fetching wife will never crack the protective barrier around his heart.

Trying to make the best of a bad marriage Louise attempts to break through the icy visage of the Marquess. But when misfortune strikes and Luke reverts to his cold, distant former self, Louise is not willing to give up on the possibility of love. After all, ice will melt when surrounded by warmth.

CHAPTER 1

Miss Louise Grant folded the last of her unmentionables and placed them into the leather traveling case that her closest friend and confidante the Duchess of Carlton—Mary to her close friends—had given to her as a parting gift. Louise slumped onto the bed, staring at the case, and fought the prickling of tears that threatened.

There was little she could do. Mary was married now and no longer in need of a companion. But it would certainly be very hard to part ways. They'd been in each other's company since Louise was eight years of age, and was sent to be a friend and companion for the young Lady Mary Dalton as she was then in Derbyshire.

The room she'd been given in the duchess's London home was now bare of trinkets and pictures she'd drawn over the years, all packed away in her trunks to be soon shipped north to a family in York. Six children awaited her there, in need of teaching and guidance and she just hoped she did well with the new position. She needed to ensure it was so since her own siblings relied on her income.

Surely it should not be so very hard to go from a lady's companion to a nursemaid and tutor. With any luck, perhaps if they were happy with her work, when Sir Daxton's eldest daughter came of age for her first Season, perchance they may employ her as a companion once more.

Certainly, she needed the stability of employment and would do everything in her power to ensure she remained with Sir Daxton's family. With two siblings to care for at her aunt's cottage in Sandbach, Cheshire, it was paramount she made a success of her new employ.

Mary bustled into the room and stopped when she spied the packed trunks. Her shoulders slumped. "Louise, you do not need to leave. Please reconsider. Married or not, you're my friend and I do not want to see you anywhere else but here."

Louise smiled, reaching out a hand to Mary. "You do not need me hanging about your skirts. You're married now, a wife, and I'm sure the duke wants you all to himself."

A blush stole over Mary's cheeks, but still she persisted, shaking her head. "You're wrong. Dale wants you to stay as much as I. Your brother and sister are well cared for by your aunt. Please do not leave us all."

Louise patted her hand, standing. As much as Louise loved her friend, Mary did not know that her aunt relied heavily on the money she made here as her companion. That without such funds their life would be a lot different than it was now. "I must leave. Sir Daxton is expecting me, so I must go." Even if the thought of leaving all that she'd known frightened her and left the pit of her stomach churning. Mary may wish her to stay, but there was nothing left for her here. Not really. Her siblings were settled, happily going to the village school and improving themselves. Sir Daxton's six children were in need of guidance and teaching and she could not let him or his wife down. They had offered to pay her handsomely, and with the few extra funds she would procure from the employment, she hoped in time to have her siblings move closer than they now were. A place that no one could rip from under them or force them to be parted again.

The memory of the bailiffs dragging her parents onto the street…her mother screaming and begging for them to give them more time. Even now she could hear her mother's wailing as they threw all their meager belongings onto the street, the townspeople simply looking on, staring and smirking at a family that had fallen low.

None of them had offered to help, and with nowhere else to go, they had moved in with her mother's sister, a widow with no children in Cheshire. The blow to the family was one that her parents could not tolerate or accept and her father took his own life, her mother only days later. Their aunt had said she had died of a broken heart, but Louise often wondered if she'd injured herself just as her papa had done.

Within days of losing her parents, Louise had been placed in a carriage and transported to Derbyshire to the Earl of Lancaster's estate. Having once worked there, her aunt still knew the housekeeper and had procured her a position through that means.

She owed a great deal to the earl's family, and her aunt. She would be forever grateful for the education, love and care they had bestowed upon her, but they had done their part in helping her. It was time she helped herself and started off in a new direction, just as Mary had done after marrying the Duke of Carlton.

"Very well." Mary's eyes glinted with unshed tears and Louise pulled her into a hug.

"We will see each other again and I will write to you every month, to tell you what is happening and how I am faring."

Mary wiped at her cheek, sniffing. "Please do. You're my best friend. A sister to me in all ways except blood. I would hate to lose you."

Louise picked up her valise and placed it on top of one of her many trunks. "Now, should we not get ready for your first London ball this evening? As the newly minted Duchess of Carlton, you must look simply perfect."

"And you too, dearest." Mary strode to the bell pull and rang for a maid. "You're going to look like a duchess as well this evening. I have not lost hope that some gentleman will fall instantly in love with you as soon as he sees you and you will never have to think of York or Sir Daxton and his six children ever again."

Louise laughed. How she would miss her friend and her never-ending hope that someone would marry her. But the chances of such a boon occurring were practically zero. She was a lady's companion, no nobility in her blood or dowry. Perhaps she would find a gentleman's son in York, a man who would love her for the small means that she did possess—a good education and friends in high places. A man who would welcome her two siblings and their impoverished state and support them as she was trying to do.

"One can only hope," she said, humoring her. "I will certainly try, if not for my own sake, then definitely for yours, Your Grace."

Mary beamed. "That is just what I like to hear. Now, what should we do with your hair…"

Want to read more? A Midsummer Kiss available now!

WAYWARD WOODVILLES
COMING SOON!

New spicy Regency romance series
Coming February 2022!
Pre-order your copy today!

SERIES BY TAMARA GILL

The Wayward Woodvilles

Royal House of Atharia

League of Unweddable Gentlemen

Kiss the Wallflower

Lords of London

To Marry a Rogue

A Time Traveler's Highland Love

A Stolen Season

Scandalous London

High Seas & High Stakes

Daughters Of The Gods

Stand Alone Books

Defiant Surrender

To Sin with Scandal

Outlaws

ABOUT THE AUTHOR

Tamara is an Australian author who grew up in an old mining town in country South Australia, where her love of history was founded. So much so, she made her darling husband travel to the UK for their honeymoon, where she dragged him from one historical monument and castle to another.

A mother of three, her two little gentlemen in the making, a future lady (she hopes) and a part-time job keep her busy in the real world, but whenever she gets a moment's peace she loves to write romance novels in an array of genres, including regency, medieval and time travel.

www.tamaragill.com
tamaragillauthor@gmail.com

Printed in Great Britain
by Amazon